MONSTERS

AND

LOLLIPOPS

BY

F.D. LINCOLN

WITH

ELIZABETH WALL PORAY

MONOGRAM PRESS

AUTHOR'S NOTE: This is a work of fiction. Names, characters, places, and incidents either are the product of the author's imagination or are used fictitiously, and any resemblance to actual persons, living or dead, business establishments, or locales is entirely coincidental.

THE MONSTER CREEPS

Inside the house, Sissy's alarm could hardly be heard by the intruder. He moved on down the hallway toward Liz's bedroom. In the silence, he could hear her breathing evenly in deep sleep.

But, somehow, even in deep sleep, the unwanted presence permeated the darkness and drifted into Liz's unconsciousness and she began to stir. Her eyeballs began to move beneath the lids. REM, rapid eye movement which accompanied her dreams. The monster began to tug at Liz's soul and she stirred with visions of shadows, demons and monsters; shaking her out of her slumber and jolting her wide awake with the pain and terror the monster always brought on. Shards of pain shot through her entire body. Her back pained and her legs were on fire. Her arms were heavy and wooden, paralyzed and useless.

Her eyes came wide open, but they ached and even in the darkness, she knew her vision was blurred. Only vague shades of blacks and grays loomed above her, but she knew there was movement in the darkness. A blob of black moved from the hallway and blocking out the grey of the bedroom doorway; a large, hulking shapeless shadow moving slowly and quietly toward her.

For

Carol Hambleton

*Don't forget us.
We won't forget you.*

In Memorium for
Ruth & John Wall

PROLOGUE

The monster was there all the time. It lurked in my shadow and waited to attack. It was there at my high school graduation. It was there at my wedding and when my son was born. It followed me to work and watched silently, patiently; ready to spring its full fury and wrath upon me. But it was a patient monster, slowly creeping up on me; slowly whittling away at my strength, gradually moving into my bones and muscles so subtly that I didn't see it coming.

The monsters initials are M.S. Multiple Sclerosis. It is a disease that strikes only the central nervous system, consisting of the brain and spinal cord. It affects the movements and functions of the entire body. The brain sends and receives signals and the spinal cord directs them throughout the body through a network of nerves. These nerves are surrounded by an insulating fatty material called myelin which forms a protective coating for the nerves during the first ten years of one's life.

When this myelin breaks down, it is replaced by scar tissue which slows down and blocks signals to and from the central nervous system to the rest of the body, severely impairing vision, strength, and coordination.

This monster crept so slyly into my life and took up a deep seated residence without my awareness. Then as time wore on, it gradually became obvious that there was something wrong with me. It first started in the eighties. I would get blurred vision in my right eye, which I blew off as staring at a computer screen too much. I didn't worry much about it.

The summer of 1989 brought numb legs and mild pain that came and went spasmodically. I ignored these symptoms too. I was in my mid thirties by then and had gone back to school to become a paralegal. I then went to work for my nephew, who had a busy, if not somewhat questionable practice. I was a go getter in those days, always working hard and putting in long hours. I blamed the onset of continuing fatigue to the stress and pressure of the job.

The early nineties brought additional pain, numb fingers, leg weakness and a tight band like feeling around my stomach. I thought all of this was strange, but I found it hard to explain to doctors. I thought I had somehow, hurt a nerve from all of the work I was doing.

In January, 1995, I was having lot of pain in my legs; not the kind of pain that goes down the back of the leg, but the whole leg. I thought this was very weird and was finding it more and more difficult to ignore what was happening to me. In April of 1995, I could not walk at all from paralysis in my right leg and numbness from the waist down. I finally had to face it, that something was very wrong.

My primary care provider sent me to a neurologist, who sent me for an MRI of brain and spinal areas. Finally, I had come face to face with the Monster. I was diagnosed with multiple sclerosis.

I was given steroids by infusion. I would go to the hospital in the city, early in the morning before work, everyday for a week. I would be placed in a recliner chair in a big open bay area with about twenty other patients who were receiving intravenous treatment of some sort.

I would have a bag containing steroids, hanging from an apparatus that would drip the right amount of medication steadily for about five hours each day. The steroid infusions took a tremendous toll on my body. It caused my arthritis to worsen and my blood pressure skyrocketed. If one part of my body hurt, it would affect everything else too.

They would leave the needle in a vein in my hand all week, so they could refasten the apparatus each day that I reported to the hospital. I would have to be careful of my every movement, for if the needle bent in the vein, it would hurt with a stabbing pain. It would be sore all week and I would have to sleep on my back in the night, by keeping my hand on my chest. If I rolled over on the hand, it would hurt so bad that it would wake me up. Nights of fitful sleep left me tired and exhausted.

I went through this hell every six months for years, just so I could go to work. I really should have stopped working years ago, but I kept on dancing with this monster inside of me. Time and time again, I went back for more infusion treatments. I gained weight each time I went through the process. I would then become depressed, followed by periods of excitable giddiness appearing happy and talkative off and on for two months following each treatment cycle. Over time, the steroids seem to help. The strength in my legs came back somewhat, and I was able to walk, however the numbness and pain remained, making it necessary to limit my activities. Paxil was prescribed to help with the pain and the depression. The doctors put me on a Hydrocodine 750 daily regimen so I could continue working.

My right leg gave out whenever I walked too much in a day. Foot drop became a fact of life for me and never went away. The pain pills, however, helped me to continue on with not only work, but just life in general.

As the nineties progressed, my multiple sclerosis also progressed. The monster upped the stakes and the dance became more horrific. My doctor sent me for more testing to determine if anything else was contributing to this unrelenting pain. I returned to the hospital for spine L/S-AP+LAT-myelogram. The tests found degenerative disease in the lumbar spine, L4, L5 encroachment, and Spondylosthesis. I was then sent to a pain management clinic. They administered a series of facet joint and epidural steroid blocks, none of which worked. I then began a regimen of stretching exercises and learned many physical therapy methods that I have since made a part of my daily routine, along with electrical stimulation from a tens unit. I even tried acupuncture for awhile. It was very painful and proved to be a very bad experience. I was stuck on the acupuncture table, unable to move. My body rejected the needles. It was a very rare reaction.

The monster was still becoming stronger. More and more it was in control of the dance. Severe pain in the leg continued and my hip continued to give out on me on an almost daily basis. I became dependent on a cane and eventually bought a wheelchair to help me through the day. I had bad fatigue which required me to take two naps a day. Blurred vision in my right eye started to come and go on a regular basis and my bowels began to have a mind of their own. I could no longer work and it became necessary to stay home most of the time.

I began to watch television a lot and read novels. I reread my collection of Nancy Drew books, which I had saved from my childhood and became enthralled with mystery stories. I became addicted to Turner Classic Movies. There was something reassuring about the old black and white movies and the stars that had been part of my life so long ago when I felt good. Especially, Bette Davis. She was my favorite. I especially liked her performance in Jezebel and her famous line; "Better fasten your seat belts. It's gonna be a bumpy ride." For some unknown reason, I always identified with her and tried to emulate her mannerisms and the clever way she had with words. I tried, but I don't think I ever fully succeeded and with the onset of the monster, I think I failed miserably and I fell into a habit of bitter and sarcastic witticism. Bette Davis was actually born Ruth Elizabeth. I always found it interesting that my mother's name was Ruth and mine was Elizabeth.

I acquired the cutest little pug puppy that I named Sissy Boom Boom. She was great company when my husband was off to work as Chief of Police of the little town of Mandalyn. She was great company and very possessive of me. She would sit on my lap while I watched the old movies. Eventually, she became so used to them that even when I was not with her, she would curl up in her chair and watch the movies without me.

In the spring of 2002, I suffered another devastating blow. This time it was not my monster that brought it on. Everyone seems to have their own monster in their life and this time my husband, Joe Porelli, met his. I suppose everyone in the law enforcement business has to acknowledge the dangers that exists and the monsters they must face, but I don't think Joe ever thought that a fate such as what befell him that day in May could have ever happened in a quiet small town where the most dangerous things he had to contend with might be a violent drunk or an out of control domestic squabble.

He had been found, barely alive, in the abandoned rock quarry north of town. The back of his head had been bashed in and a bloody rock was found next to him.

There were no suspects and no clue as to the assailant or assailants. There was no clue as to why Joe was there in the quarry. Joe eventually regained consciousness but his dementia was such that he was no longer cognizant of his surrounding or any one around him. It had been necessary to commit him to a nursing home ten miles away, just south of Buffalo.

Along with my own illness, the added burden of nursing home expenses, threatened to bankrupt us financially. Unbeknownst to me, Joe had fortunately, had the foresight to set up a trust fund to take care of me in case of something happening to him. My nephew Michael, the attorney that I had previously worked for had helped Joe set it up with money that Joe had supposedly, won at the local racetrack. Neither Michael nor Joe had ever told me about this, for they knew how I felt about gambling and about Joe's brother, Vinnie, who was reputed to be a gangland boss and heavy into the gambling world.

I was now alone and the Monster took advantage of it. I became more depressed and despondent. I could barely function and could no longer care for myself. It soon became obvious that I could no longer live alone.

The answer to my loneliness came in the form of a wild, fun loving, bundle of dynamite named Deb Raymond. She came whirling into my life astride a Red Honda Rebel Motorcycle, having just discarded her third husband and looking for a new life.

I had known Deb all my life. Actually she was my aunt, even though she was a full five years my junior, but that's another story, in itself.

She came to live with me and became my helpmate. She got a job as a waitress, serving the counter at a local restaurant, 'The Gossip Grill'. And when she wasn't working she was helping me.

In time my life began to stabilize and I learned to deal better with the monster. Deb was an adventure all to herself and her whimsies began to rub off on me. It soon became obvious; it was time to fasten the seat belts. I knew from then on, it was going to be a bumpy ride.

October 1989

A short blast of sooty exhaust puffed from the tailpipe, followed by clean fumes as the engine revved, the tires gripped the dirt track, spewing the reddish dust behind the treads and sending the red Ford 4x4 pickup truck, forward. The winged racing gates folded to the sides of the pickup bed as the vehicle sped away from the trailing pack of horses and sulkies, signaling the beginning of the race.

The tall brilliant night lights that loomed above the track and the club house stands, cast a surreal glow over the raceway. Misty fog hovered like haloes around the lights as the heat from them turned the crisp fall night air into lingering translucent clouds. The crowd began to roar as the horses abruptly lurched forward; each one trying to get a head start on the others. Whips snapped, cart wheels whirred and leather tracings crackled. Hoofs pounded out a steady staccato of stabbing drum beats into the loose dirt of the track as the horses legs moved laterally, right front and right behind, then left front and left hind legs striking the ground simultaneously, for these were pacers. Trotting horses had raced early on in the evening, but this was the final race of the day; the main event for pacers and a mile long run for the eight entries. The jockeys leaned back on the bikes between the two large bicycle wheels; their legs spread far apart on the forward bars. Silk colors of red, blues, greens, orange, yellow and all their combinations flashed in the light from above as the participants rolled past the spectators in the stands, and jockeyed for position.

Shards of light reflected off their goggles that were snugged tightly to the driver's faces protecting them from the wind and horses' tails that streamed out behind them as they increased the speed.

The announcer's voice was muted in the overhead speakers as he rattled off the changing lineup, exuding as much excitement as he could to keep the audience thrilled. Out of the gate, the drivers were all vying for the lead, then as they tried to avoid being boxed in, they seemed to separate into two lines--one on the rail and one on the outside.

Nightshade Rajah, a sleek black in the purple colors, raced to the front on the outside in a first over position, ahead of the others, taking an early lead with an initial burst of speed, followed by Sundown Courage, Ruling Prince, Whitewater George, Ebenezar, Quarter Moon, Vivatar and Kentucky Flower,   At the turn and into the second quarter mile, Sundown Courage pulled in behind Nightshade Rajah, racing with cover on the outside, while Ruling Prince rolled in along the rail, claiming the pocket and securing a garden trip. Whitewater George and Ebenezar swung wide to the outside; the jockey pulling sharply to the right and sneaking him in front of Whitewater George. Quarter Moon, Vivatar and Kentucky Flower continued along the rail with Vivatar caught in the death hole as the third position on the rail; a spot difficult to break out of.

As they neared the far turn in the third quarter mile, Ruling Prince had moved ahead on the rail, edging ahead of Nightshade Rajah, Whitewater George had broken away from Ebenzar and pulling ahead of him to close in on the leader. Kentucky Flower was quickly losing stamina and had fallen back far to the rear, allowing Vivatar the room he needed to break out of the death hole and pull to the outside, increasing speed and closing in on the three lead horses. The jockey, repeatedly, struck his whip across the sulky shaft, making noise to urge Vivatar onward. The line of horses and bikes, almost side by side in front of him held him back from breaking through.

As they entered the final quarter mile it was a three way race. Vivatar was still barred from moving up and the others had fallen back, totally out of contention. All three horses battled it out with increasing speed; each one momentarily taking the lead and then another.

The crowd was going wild. Cheers and yells filled the crisp night air and the announcer's voice was drowned out. The noise reached a new level as Whitewater George broke stride and started to gallop. The jockey immediately hauled back on the leathers, slowing the horse and pulling to the outside, trying to force him to regain his stride.

It only took a few moments, but the break was enough to allow Vivatar to pull through the opening and draw abreast of Nightshade Rajah and Ruling Prince. Whitewater George pulled back into the track trapped in Vivatar's old spot.

As they neared the finish, Nightshade Rajah started to lose ground. Ruling Prince pulled forward to take the lead with Vivatar close behind by a half length. Coming into the stretch, it was Ruling Prince by a neck, then by a nose, and as they flashed passed the finish line, the crowd was screaming with wonder. Photo finish! The crowd would not know the results until the judges had ruled.

When the results were finally announced, Vivatar was proclaimed the winner. The unknown horse; the longest shot of the day had brought in the money.

The darkness of the night and the silence left by the absence of the crowd cast an eeriness over the clubhouse and grounds. The brilliant track lights were extinguished now, leaving the track in deep shadow behind the club house. Lights from inside the building were burning bright and floodlights lit the grounds in front of the clubhouse.

The armored car pulled into the circular drive and stopped by the awning covered walkway that led into the front entrance. The driver shifted into reverse and backed into a driveway that paralleled the walkway, and stopped a few feet from a pair of steel double doors and killed the engine.

The uniformed driver and his attendant guard hopped from the cab with pistols drawn. They moved to the rear of the vehicle and swung the back panel doors open. The two iron doors to the clubhouse swung open and were held secured in place by two uniformed track security men. Six more security guards followed through the opening; two going to each side of the walkway and two went to the front of the truck, to stand guard. All were armed. More security guards lined the hallway inside the club house as two more security men carried heavy metal containers to the armored car and lifted them inside. They returned to the clubhouse two more times until they had loaded a total of six containers.

The entire operation took but a few minutes. When all was secured, the driver and attendant climbed aboard and drove off into night with the day's receipts as usual. But, there was something different about this pickup. The driver smiled coyly at his companion as they drove off down the road. Neither said anything to the other for a full ten minutes. Behind them, the hulking shape of the raceway clubhouse faded into the distance, blending into the lonely stretch of empty land surrounding it, for it had been built in a rural section, far from any busy towns or cities. After three miles of straight driving, the armored car came to a stop at a four way stop sign. The driver looked in all directions. As usual, there was no traffic at this time of night on such a lonely stretch of road. The land spread out in a flat plain in all directions.

Here, the armored car always made a left turn, heading toward Buffalo. But tonight, the driver chuckled as he whipped the wheel to the right, stepped on the gas and drove speedily toward a different destination.

After a mile, the truck turned left onto a narrow winding dirt road that led back into a wooded area which hugged both sides of the road. The truck bounced on its springs as it dropped into chuck holes and bounded over rocks of varying shapes and sizes. Speed was greatly diminished at this point, but eventually the road smoothed out as it emerged from the trees. A little further on, the truck pulled over to the right through what appeared to be a patch of tall grass, but as the vehicle negotiated the turn, it was obvious that here was a two rutted tractor path leading down into a valley surrounded by high wooded hills. The trail wound downward until the truck emerged into a clear meadow which had the remnants of a mowed hayfield.

The armored car came to a halt in the meadow. The engine went silent and the headlights went out. From across the meadow, two head lights came on momentarily and then went out. Two more times, they flashed. The armored car's lights came on once again, then off, then on again. Then went black.

The sound of an engine starting across the field broke the stillness of the late night air. Then, the headlights came back on and stayed on this time. The armored car driver and his companion smiled to each other; their excitement growing by the second as they watched the oncoming headlights approaching; two golden orbs in the darkness bouncing about as the coming vehicle negotiated the rough terrain.

From the top of the hill to the east, a lone hunter sat at the edge of the woods. He had one boot off and he was rubbing the blister on his left foot. The boots were new and hardly broken in. He had been tramping these woods for several hours with two companions, who had gone on without him, while he cooled his foot. The dogs had treed a raccoon someplace deeper into the woods and his friends had headed off toward the barking.

As the hunter started to put his sock back on, he saw head lights of a vehicle descending into the meadow below. More hunters? He thought. Pretty late at night to just be starting out. Maybe they had been hunting elsewhere and decided to try their luck around here.

He watched as he smoothed his sock into place and lifted his boot. The vehicle rolled to the floor of the valley and stopped. The lights went out. The hunter was beginning to lace his boot when he saw the headlights flash across the field. The first vehicle returned the flash and the second vehicle rolled forward.

Odd! The hunter thought. He picked up his .30-.30 shotgun and crawled further out of the woods to get a better vantage point.

From the beams of each of the vehicle's headlights, the hunter could finally make out the shape of an armored car and a pick up truck. What the hell was an armored car doing out here? He crawled forward again, peering into the darkness.

He watched while two men emerged from the cab of the armored car and another got out of the pickup. He heard the men laugh as they greeted each other, but their conversation was muted by the distance and he couldn't make out what they were saying.

After the brief greeting the three men got to work. The two men from the armored car opened the rear panel doors while the other man lowered the tailgate to the pickup. He then stepped aside and let the armored car men do all the work of unloading metal containers, carrying them to the pick up, and placing them in the bed of the truck.

When they were finished moving the containers, the pickup truck driver climbed into the back of the truck and rearranged the load and spread a canvas over it. One of the armored car men went to the cab and came back to his partner, who held his hands out toward him wrists together. What the....? It looked like the one man was wrapping something around the other one's wrist. Duct tape! He was wrapping duck tape! Then the man was on the ground and his legs were being wrapped with it.

The man from this pick up, hopped down and took the duck tape from the standing armored car man, who now held his wrists out, while his wrists were wrapped. Then he too sat on the ground while his legs were wrapped.

They're robbing the armored car, themselves! The hunter thought to himself. And they're making it look like they were robbed! But wait, what's that?

The pickup man had returned to his truck and retrieved something from inside the cab. He left the driver's side door open as he strode back toward the two men on the ground. In the beams of headlights, the hunter could see the man was carrying a rifle or shotgun. It was too hard to see from this distance.

The man raised the weapon to his shoulder, aiming down at his two accomplices. The hunter could hear the excited protests from the bound men as they realized what was happening. A double cross!

The weapon boomed twice, recoiling against the man's shoulder. A shotgun, the hunter realized. His heart pounded and he could hardly believe his eyes. The two forms on the ground went limp. A silence replaced the booming echoes that died out across the meadow.

The shooter went to the armored car, reached through the window on the driver side door and extinguished the head lights. He now became a shadow moving back to his truck. He tossed the shotgun onto the seat and climbed in after it. The engine kicked into life and the truck drove off.

The hunter continued to watch as the truck navigated its way up the same track that the armored car had taken down into the valley. From his vantage point, on the high hill, the hunter watched as the headlights disappeared into a wooded area. A moment later, the headlights reappeared on the road above. The truck turned right and continued on; its tail lights gleaming red in the darkness.

A short distance down the road, the vehicle turned and the lights disappeared from view once again for several seconds. The light of the head-lights winked again through the darkness. Then again. The truck appeared to be on a winding route that descended downward.

An old abandoned quarry was in that direction! The thief must be going down into it, the hunter thought to himself.

CHAPTER ONE

It had been four and a half years since Liz Porelli had her last infusion treatment and as she anticipated her current treatment, the memories of those infusions came back to her, as if it had been only yesterday. This time she would not be getting the steroid treatment. This would be a new experience, although the infusion process would be much the same.

She had been reluctant to agree to the treatment when Doctor Callan first suggested it. It was strictly an experimental treatment. If it worked as predicted, motor function control could be managed somewhat with less pain, enabling the MS patient to have more so called "good days" over an extended period of time. The drug had not yet been named. For the time being it was referred to as AXB4.

Liz had dismissed the thought of any experimental treatment, but when doctor Callan pointed out that she could be doing a service for other multiple sclerosis sufferers, as well as potentially improving the quality of her own life, she finally agreed to the treatment. Liz liked Doctor Callan.

He was young, but he seemed competent and Liz had known his father, Martin Callan, who ran the local farm equipment store in Mandalyn, for many years. He had been a good friend of her husband, Joe, and had often accompanied him on hunting and fishing trips, but that was several years ago now.

As she checked into Amity Hospital, early that morning, her apprehension grew and beckoned the return of the monster as stressful situations often did. The pain in her leg seemed to be screaming at her, the vision in her right eye was blurring, and her footing was unsteady, even with the help of the four pronged bottomed cane she leaned on as she made her way from the waiting area to the infusion room.

It still looked the same as when Liz had been here before; just a little dingier, a little less bright, and more cluttered with usage. It still had that hot, stale, antiseptic air, mixed with the smell of disinfectant detergent.

As Liz made her way down the hallway, she passed the open closet area for hanging coats and jackets. There was no door on it. She thought about stopping and hanging up her brown suede jacket, but decided against it. She just didn't feel that comfortable with hospital security. She decided she would stack the jacket, as usual, on the pile with her other belongings; her purse, a book, and a magazine, next to her infusion chair, where even though close to her, they could disappear if she went to sleep during the process. Such happenings had occurred many times with other patients and once to her. Today she had brought an extra bag with her containing three sweat suits which were now too small for her. She would leave them on the coffee table in the center of the infusion room and tell everyone that they were there for the taking.

On her right, Liz passed by the nursing station partitioned off from the main infusion room by a half height wall with a foot high window running the full length of the partition. Liz noted her reflection in the glass. Her normally curled and puffed hair was frizzy from the early morning breeze outside. The once dark auburn hair seemed much lighter as the bits of gray ends peeked through the curl. Getting frumpy looking, she thought to herself, as she saw her reflection which was distorted by the angle of glass and light, making her look shorter and chubbier than she really was, for she was fairly tall and carried herself well, despite hunching over a cane.

There were two nurses sitting at two of the three desks, behind the partition. The third desk was empty, but the chair was rolled away, indicating that the third nurse was somewhere around but not in the station currently. She was probably one of the three attendees roaming about the infusion room, setting up procedures and keeping a constant watch on each patient's progress. Two of them wore purple uniforms and one wore a white one. The one in white was obviously the nurse; a different one than she had seen here on the previous days. And the other two were merely attendants; only one had been on duty during Liz's other visits. She had not seen the young black girl before.

The room was a big open bay area with padded lounge style chairs spaced along three walls. There were twenty of these chairs and patients of both sexes, various ages, walks of life and social status, occupied these chairs with very little privacy. Each chair had an overhead light for reading and an accompanying transom equipped with apparatus for varying types of intravenous treatments, requiring constant monitoring. The procedures were the same for everyone; only the kind of medication administered was different. While some patients might be receiving potassium, others might be receiving chemo, steroids, vitamin B12, or experimental drugs, through a translucent bag that hung from the transom and fed intravenously into the patient's arm.

Liz dropped her package of old clothes off on the coffee table as she passed by and found her way to her usual chair which was the third one from the right corner of the far wall next to the rest rooms and a large garbage can. A middle aged man with thin balding gray hair pulled back into a spindly pony tail, and dressed in blue scrubs was emptying the can into a barrel like container on rollers. He wheeled it away leaving a sticky chocolate covered ice cream wrapper behind on the floor. He backed the cart up and then went forward again. He ran over the wrapper with the wheels of his cart. The wrapper stuck to one of the wheels and there it stayed, going around and around with each cycle.

Several patients were already seated along the adjacent wall. Some had already started their infusions and others were still waiting to start. Other patients were still coming in behind Liz.

Liz stacked her belongings against the wall next to her chair and eased herself into it. Her arm throbbed with pain where the needle in her vein was still placed from the previous treatment and available for use today. There was a large black, blue, purplish bruise around the needle site.

There was a large map of the U.S on the wall. It had been a subject for idle conversation, the first day she came for treatment. It seemed odd to be the only decorative item in the otherwise austere room. There was a table model television on a plain white wooden table beneath it.

Many of the patients were watching Good Morning America while others merely sat or dozed in their chairs. Four patients were gathered along the left wall; their chairs turned slightly inward to form a half semi quarter circle of sorts. Three were women and one was a flabby old man with a gray beard and mustache. They were playing cards, while waiting for their procedures to start.

To Liz's left, a thin middle aged man with thinning dark hair was talking to a much younger man with a full head of shaggy black hair and a scruffy beard that appeared to be more like several days of stubble rather than an actual beard.

The younger man had been boasting about having ten children, while the older man lamented very openly about his inabilities to have any. Both were very vocal and boisterous, ignoring Liz's presence, or anyone else's, for that matter, and being very graphic in their conversation.

Over against the right wall, kitty corner from where Liz sat, a lady in a U.S. Army uniform sat next to a young man. The lady was probably in her late thirties and the rank showing on her uniform collar identified her as Lieutenant Colonel. The young man was thin shouldered, short and bony. He had a silver ring protruding from his left nostril and a series of three varied colored rings, pinched around each eyebrow. There was a faded imprint of a rebel flag on the front of his dirty tee shirt.

The lady Colonel was explaining the advantages the United States Army had available to the boy. He merely scoffed at the thought of it, but it didn't deter the lady from continuing to try to influence him.

On the other side of the young man, sat a middle aged woman with obviously dyed red hair, framing her lean face with long strands that tumbled across her shoulders. Aging wrinkles seemed to appear more prominent against the obvious attempt to look younger. She wore a beautiful Cashmere sweater and there were expensive rings on her fingers. She obviously was a lady of means and wealth and was totally uncomfortable with these surroundings and having to associate with the lower echelons of society. She held her chin high and remained aloof, not caring to converse with anyone else. This was the first day Liz had seen this patient, and she was occupying the same chair that another lady across the room had occupied the day before.

To her left sat an older woman in a pudding stained yellow shirt. Her straight, gray streaked, unkempt black hair hung in greasy, dirty clumps around the folds of a thick neck. She had worn the same pudding stained shirt and the same torn jeans as she had on the previous days Liz had been there. Liz saw her keep glancing toward the table where she had left the package.

"I left some clothes in that bag on the coffee table," Liz announced to the room, but she was making sure the pudding stained woman understood. "Anyone who can use them; feel free to take them," she said.

The pudding stained woman glanced away quickly as if not interested, but occasionally, Liz would see her cast a furtive glance toward the package.

The cashmere sweater lady only rolled her eyes in disgust and if she could have wrinkled her nose, she probably would have.

Liz was still watching the others around her when the young black attendant rolled a transom next to her on the left. "How are you today?" She said in a light, cheerful tone.

"Fine," Liz lied, for she was feeling most uncomfortable with the needle in her vein and her leg was paining fitfully. Her head leaned back

against the chair's head rest and she rolled her
eyes upward to see the attendant. Even with her
blurred vision, Liz could see that the aide was
very attractive. She was short and slender with a
good figure and her face was oval shaped, with
sharp features that were very striking, with large
black lashes curving above the dark eyes. She
had a warm and genuine smile. She couldn't have
been more than twenty one. Liz tried to make out
the name tag, but she couldn't focus on it through
the blurred fog of her vision.

"My name is Celia," the aide said. "I'll be attending to you this morning, Ms......" She
checked Liz's chart that she had clamped to a clip
board. "Ms., Mrs. Porelli?" she said as if verify-
ing she had the correct patient.

Liz often wondered how they kept everyone
straight, here in the infusion room. Patients were
constantly moving around and changing chair
positions.   If the attendants kept track of
numbered chair positions instead of by patient's
name, the results could be disastrous and the
wrong patients could be getting the wrong
treatments. Knowing her luck, Liz never wanted
to take any chances, so she always made sure she
took the same chair on each visit and she stayed
with it until the entire procedure was over.

"Yes, that's right," Liz said. "But call me Liz.
Mrs. makes me feel old and worthless and Ms.
makes me feel women's libbish, if they still use
that term. I never did subscribe to that crap. I

never wanted to be a man's equal. I was always happy to just be his better."

Celia smiled. "No, I don't think they use that term anymore," she said as she began to fit the transom apparatus and attach the infusion bag.

"Honey," Liz said. "Do me a favor, will you. And go easy attaching that tube. The needle in my vein is killing me."

"That is a nasty bruise," Celia said, lifting Liz's wrist gently and examining the needle site. She moved the needle a bit and Liz winced with the pain. The pain lasted only a brief moment and then eased significantly. "There. That should be better" she added.

"Much," Liz said gratefully. "What did you do?"

"It wasn't inserted properly. Whoever did it originally, wasn't careful."

"It was that one over there," Liz said, pointing her chin toward the other aide.

Celia grimaced. "That's Shirley. She shouldn't even be working here. She's lazy and takes too many shortcuts. She doesn't care about the patients. She's just here for a paycheck." She attached the tube to the needle and adjusted the liquid flow from the infusion bag.

"Then I'm glad I have you today, Celia," Liz said. She glanced upward and saw the medication start to drip into the tube. She started to think of all the times she had been there and all the nurses she had talked to. For twenty five years she had returned to the hospital. The same sick smells that overwrought the rooms were still here.

Celia smiled, "You just relax, now," she said. "I'll be back to check on you later."

"Thank you," Liz said, settling back in her chair and watching her cross the room to the woman in the cashmere sweater.

Liz leaned back and rested for a few minutes. The activity in the room, as more and more patients were prepared, soon weighed on Liz's energy. Just the sight of such hustle and bustle tired her. She leaned back, trying to get more comfortable, but lying on her back was never a good position for her. She could always rest best when sleeping in her bed and on her stomach.

She watched the steady drip, drip of the medication for several minutes. She felt fidgety and tired all at the same time. She started to count the drops and when she reached a hundred, she continued to count them. But as a countdown, this time, counting backwards from one hundred to zero. She did this two times and somewhere during the third countdown she fell asleep.

When she awoke, the room was filled with excitement. As she gradually wiped the sleep from her eyes, she began to focus in on the scene before her. Her blurred vision was gone and she could see clearly now.

The nurses and attendants and several resident doctors were congregated in the area where the cashmere sweater lady had been sitting. Liz couldn't see what was happening, but the residents were hovered over her.

"What's going on?" Liz asked to no one in particular, looking to her left at the man next to her and to her right toward the military lady.

"Well, I'm only hearing whispers, but I think she died," the Lieutenant Colonel said. "I think she got the wrong medication."

"Who?"

"The lady in the cashmere sweater. I think they said her name was Mrs. Porelli?"

"What?" Liz exclaimed. She felt of herself all over. "This is ridiculous," she said. "Every morning I feel like I wake up dead. And now I wake up dead and it's no different. Wait'll I tell Deb. She'll never believe this one."

Chapter Two

A slim, young woman slipped through the doorway into the hall and closed the door silently behind her. There was an eeriness about the empty hallway at two thirty in the morning. The building lights were kept on all night and even though there was no change in the wattage, the lights seemed less bright than when the building was bustling with normal hour's activity. The loneliness of the night hung in the air like a heavy fog with an almost ghostlike menace to it.

She clutched the gray canvas bag with the two blue straps, tightly to her body as she hurried down the medical center hallway toward the elevators at the south end of the wing. Her rubber soled nursing shoes padded against the tile floor and echoed dully in the emptiness of the hallway.

Her breathing was short and shallow and her heart was beating rapidly; half with excitement and half with fear. She had gotten what she had come here for and the revelation of her finding was more than she had hoped for. She shifted the bag to her bosom and held it tight against her with both arms, as if protecting a baby.

She paused at the elevators and pushed the up button. She waited for what seemed like the longest half minute of her life. She could hear the elevator starting from a floor below. To her right, a large rain streaked window filled the upper half of the outside wall. Had she looked in its direction she would have seen herself in the reflection. She would have seen an attractive young lady of medium height, and in her early thirties. Her long dark brown hair hung loose and long over the shoulders of the light gray raincoat that was fully buttoned up to the neck, hiding her slender body.

The elevator car rolled to a halt. A clear bell like ding sounded as it arrived. The young lady waited with expectancy and apprehension as the door began to slide open. Her breath caught for a second, and then she let it out with relief as she realized the car was empty, as it should be at this time of night, but considering her presence here and what she had just done, she had dreaded the worst.

She quickly stepped inside and pushed the button for the fifth floor. She was currently on the second. The door slid shut and the elevator mechanism engaged once again. She felt the slight jolt as the car began to move.

She waited expectantly for the car to halt at its destination and the door slid open once again. She felt momentary relief as she saw an empty hallway, here on the fifth floor. She stepped out quickly, cast a glance down the length of the hallway, to the right. It was empty. She hustled along the corridor for about twenty feet, where another hallway seemed to branch out to the right. She turned into it and found it was also empty. It was not actually a hallway but an enclosed walkway leading from the medical center building to the main hospital complex. The sound of the drumming rain on the peaked metal roof was magnified in the silence of the night. Rivulets of rainwater streamed down the windowed sides of the walkway, distorting the lights of the night outside. The front of the hospital was brightly lighted and its reflection shimmered in the pools of water, covering the half circle driveway that curved close to the entrance. Through the glass wall to her left, a myriad of distorted city lights dotted the darkness in the distance. To her right, through the glass, she saw tall trees swaying in the whipping wind and shaking spicules of water from their mid fall withering leaves.

Her pace quickened as she neared the far end of the walkway, where it opened into the hospital wing. Sounds of movement and activity emanated from around the corner. As she emerged from the walkway, she could see a bank of elevators off to her left almost directly in front of her. The elevator doors were painted blue and a plaque on the wall clearly identified them as the 'Blue Elevators'. Directly above this plaque was a slightly larger one that said "Geriatric Wing'.

There was a cleaning woman mopping the hall-way floor, to her right. Open doored rooms lined the corridor on the far side. And, as the name of the wing indicated, the rooms were all occupied with elderly patients.

She hurried to the elevator bank and pushed the down button. Again she waited, expectantly, hearing the elevator make its way up the shaft. It came to a halt and the door opened before her. Luck was still with her. It was empty. She hur-ried inside, pushed the button for floor two; the lobby floor. The door closed and the car started downward. A few seconds later the car stopped on the fourth floor. She knew someone would be getting on. Her heart beat picked up the tempo. She hugged the bag tighter and higher, lowering her head as if she could hide behind it.

The door slid open and a short, thin, male resi-dent doctor, obviously of Hindu descent, stepped in. He was still in scrubs and a stethoscope hung loosely about his dark skinned neck. He pushed the button for floor one, without even glancing toward the woman. The door slid shut and the car continued. The lighted number above the door indicated passing floor three uneventfully. The car stopped at floor two, which was the main lobby floor. The door slid open once again.

The woman quickly hurried out into the hall-way, keeping her head down, but fully aware that the young resident's eyes were upon her. She heard the door slide shut behind her and the car continued on as she rounded the corner of the hallway into a long corridor that extended toward

the rear of the hospital in one direction and toward the lobby at the front of the hospital, in the
other direction. She hurried toward the lobby, the
sound of her heels on the corridor floor clicking
in her ears and her heart beating a throb to her
head.

The corridor emptied out into the lobby.
Lighting was dim this time of night and the lobby
was almost empty, save for two patrons keeping a
vigil for whoever they had here in the hospital.
An elderly man was stretched out on a couch
against the far wall to the left. A woman, probably his wife sat slouched in an overstuffed chair.
Her head was against the back cushion and the
side of her face lolled against the thick fabric.
Her eyes were closed. Toward the front of the
lobby, near the front doors and off to the left, a
small room was filled with bright light. This was
the security office. She tried not to look in that
direction, but occasionally she cast a furtive
glance as she passed the empty reception desk to
her right and headed toward the entrance.

The revolving door sandwiched between the
two obligatory stationary doors had obviously
been locked for the night, so she hurried toward
the door on the right, opened it and stepped into
the walkway that ran the entire length of the hospital's front wall. She jumped with startle as the
sliding glass door leading to the drive up circle
and front parking lot, outside slid open, activated
by an electric eye or motion detector of some
sort, before her, letting in a blast of cold wet au-

tumn air. She turned quickly to her right and hurried along the corridor toward the ramp garage that lay beyond the exit door at the end of the walkway. The sliding glass door buzzed shut behind her as she moved away declining to access it.

Her pace slowed and she almost halted when she heard the voice behind her. "Have a good evening," the security guard called to her. Trying not to show nervousness, she resumed her pace, fighting the urge to run. The doorway seemed such a long way off and her feet felt heavy as lead. Had the guard seen her plainly enough to remember her? No, she told herself. She had kept her head down. But, could she be sure? Her heartbeat raced even faster and her breathing was tight.

Then suddenly, she was through the door and stepped into the brightly lit, but shadowed ramp garage. The door closed behind her with an echoing clang. She halted briefly, let out a sigh of relief and caught her breath. Then she hurried out into the almost empty chasm of the ramp garage. Her shoes clicked against the pavement and echoed. The hospital had been built on a hill and the ramp garage extended downward two flights as well as upward for another three.

She had left her car on the first level and she hurried along the ramp floor as it curved downward. She had just rounded the first curve, when she thought she heard it. She came up short, halting and listening. She looked about and forced herself to look behind her. It must have been her imagination she thought. She started forward again and stopped once more. No. She had not imagined it. She had heard it. It was not just the echo of her footsteps, but the echo of another set of shoes. Heavier and louder than her own. They had sounded when she moved and silenced when she stopped. Someone else was in the garage and he was following her. She quickened her pace and she heard the other footsteps quicken also. She started to run, not even trying to hold back the panic that was overtaking her. Only the sound of her own labored breathing and the clickety clack of her own shoes remained in her ears, drowning out all other sounds and losing track of the following footfalls. To the bottom floor of the ramp she ran, almost stumbling over her own feet. Finally she saw her gray Hyundai parked against the far wall of the garage. It seemed such a long ways away and her leaden legs seemed to move in slow motion until she practically slid into the side of the car door.

Quickly she fumbled in her purse for her keys. Her heart was pounding loudly in her brain and she panicked as she failed to find the keys at first. Then there they were. Her fingers curled about them and she pulled them feverishly from the bag. Her hands trembled and she dropped the keys. They clinked to the concrete floor. She reached for them almost dropping the bag containing what she had taken from the medical center, but she managed to retain her grasp, while retrieving the keys and trying once more to insert the correct one in the lock.

Once, twice, she tried and failed, but then she managed to unlock the door. She banged the door against her left knee as she jumped behind the wheel and slammed it shut. Her finger found the automatic lock button and she thrust it forward. The sound of the locks engaging into place assured her she was safe. She breathed a little easier with relief. She checked out the area through each side window. There was no movement about the garage. Perhaps she had been imagining things, she told herself, but she still turned the ignition with an urgency and cranked the engine into life. The tires squealed and echoed loudly within the confines of the garage as she backed out of her parking spot, slammed on the brakes and threw the stick into drive. She wheeled sharply to the left and stomped on the gas. Again the wheels squealed as she sent the vehicle forward at an accelerating speed toward the exit.

The toll booth was closed as it usually was this time of night and the guard rail gate was up. The Hyundai rolled rapidly through the opening, navigated the winding drive that led down the hill toward the street below. She turned right onto the street and rolled toward the main intersection. There was a stop light here and it was red, but she didn't want to stop. She flicked on the wipers to clear away the rain and she glanced left and right making sure there was no traffic. She rolled on through the light, twisting the wheel sharply to the left, turning south, then straightening out the wheel as she applied pressure to the accelerator and driving off into the darkness.

As she approached cruising speed she began to relax. Her breathing began to ease and she felt a sudden rush of relief. Safe. She thought without realizing a shadowy shape was rising from the back seat.

Chapter Three

"How do I look, Liz?" Deb Raymond shouted from her perch.

"Like a damn fool, as usual," Liz Porelli answered. "Only higher off the ground." Deb ignored the jab and continued to play with the steering wheel of the John Deere tractor that she was sitting on. Her long oval face was screwed up in a delighted grin; her wide mouth stretched upward at the ends and seemed to spread from ear to ear. She uttered 'varoom, varoom' sounds between her teeth and worked the steering wheel back and forth like a child playing driver. Deb liked to have fun and she liked to play.Today Deb was playing farmer, dressed in bib overalls. Her legs were tucked inside high topped rubber boots that had been pulled over her shoes and buckled tight by five gate like, hinged fasteners on each boot. She wore a red checked flannel shirt and her long black hair hung loose beneath a matching farmer's cap. A red bandanna was fastened V shape around her skinny neck.

"Why don't you quit playing with it and start it up, you damn fool?" Liz shouted; a trace of chuckle in her voice. She reached inside the pocket of her brown, heavy polyester sweater and pulled out a Tootsie Roll Pop. She noted it was grape; one of her favorites.

"Oh, can I?" Deb asked excitedly, like a child, her dark eyes looming large with excitement behind her round framed glasses.

"We bought it. It's yours. Of course you can drive it." Liz smiled to herself, but tried to keep an indignant expression outwardly. She removed the paper from her pop and shoved the purplish ball into her mouth forming a bulge in her left cheek. She absently rolled the paper into a tiny ball between her thumb and forefinger. Then, dropped it in her sweater pocket.

Deb bobbed excitedly, up and down in the tractor's seat and rubbed her hands together in delighted anticipation. She glanced around the dashboard, locating the instruments. She found the ignition key and twisted it eagerly. The engine cranked, then turned over and sputtered into life with a bellowing clatter. Deb giggled gleefully and clapped her hands together. She glanced around, found, the clutch, brake and gas pedals; placing a foot on each in succession, measuring the length of her short legs against the reach provided by the tractor. She had to slide forward to the front of the seat in order to reach, but she seemed satisfied.

She found the gear shift stick, shoved the clutch pedal to the floor, slipped the stick into first gear, and let off on the clutch. She let it out too fast and the shiny green tractor lurched forward, taking Deb by surprise and jolting her further back into the seat. Overcoming her initial surprise, she scrambled forward on the seat, her right foot searching for the brake and her hands gripping the steering wheel in a death grip, as the tractor rolled somewhat out of control, wobbling back and forth on it huge rear tires with the wide set front wheels weaving from side to side, like a giant grasshopper, as it headed toward where Liz was standing in the parking lot of Callan's Farm Equipment dealership.

Liz tried to sidestep out of the way, difficult as it was to move with the quad cane she had been leaning on, but she was too slow and barely moved aside, needlessly, as the tractor whizzed past her in a gush of rushing air; Deb laughing and whooping her delight as she straightened out the wheel, shoved the accelerator to the floor, pushed in the clutch and shifted into second, drove off across the parking lot, turning the corner of the dealership store and disappearing into the open land behind the building.

"Looks like she's happy with it," Stan Kraus said as he stepped up behind Liz.

"If she liked it anymore, she probably would have run me over for sure," Liz said, taking the pop out of her mouth and turning to the salesman that had just sold them the tractor. He was a squat middle aged man with a receding hairline that went so far back you might as well say he was bald. His round face was ruddy and he had a jovial twinkle in his eyes.

"Sorry, I couldn't have given you a better deal on it, Liz. But, Martin couldn't see his way clear to cut the price any. However, we did give you some great discounts on the big garden rototiller attachment, so you can grow your own pumpkins next year."

Martin Callan was the owner of the dealership and had once been a good friend of Liz's husband, Joe. But that had been a long time ago, before Joe's injury. Liz had had little contact with Martin over the years, but Martin's son Roger was her Doctor and Liz held him in high esteem, even after the episode with the experimental drug for MS became a disaster. She always thought that Roger did his best with the information he was given by the pharmaceutical representatives that visited him regularly.

"I'm sure he did the best he could," Liz said.

"We can deliver it on Thursday, if you like."

"That'd be fine," Liz said absently, without looking at him, and shoving the Tootsie Pop back in her mouth as she was craned her neck to see if she could catch a glimpse of Deb and her new toy, in the field beyond. The light breeze teased at the curls of her hair and offered a hint of autumn chill in the sunshine of this beautiful Indian summer day.

"But if I know Deb, she'll want to drive it home."

"I'm sure she would," Stan agreed. "But you're not allowed to drive it on the road."

"That wouldn't bother Deb any, but the last thing this world needs is Deb turned loose on the highways with a tractor. It's bad enough she's loose on the road with our Cherokee, much less those damned motorcycles of hers."

As if on queue, the tractor came barreling around the far corner of the building. The engine clamored loudly in their ears as Deb came flying past them. The tires squealed and the Deere slewed from side to side as she braked to a sudden halt, with the tires sliding across the asphalt pavement, leaving rubber tire tread marks etched indelibly into the surface of the parking lot. Deb cut the engine and bobbed up and down on the seat, once again clapping her hands with satisfaction.

She bounded from the seat to the ground and ran excitedly, like a child toward Liz.

"Oh, I love it! I just absolutely, totally love it! Can I drive it home?" She bubbled.

"See what I told you," Liz said to Stan. He nodded with a grin.

"No you can't," Liz said to Deb sternly. "You can't drive that thing on the highway."

"Why not? I can drive anywhere. Didn't you see how good I could drive it just now?"

"Yeah, I saw it and it should be illegal for you to drive it anywhere. Unfortunately, it's only illegal on the road."

"I've seen farmer's driving equipment on the road. Some of them are much bigger than my tractor."

"Yeah, and you curse them out every time you get behind one of them. And it's still illegal."

"Well, that's 'cause they go so darn slow. I drive fast."

Stan and Liz looked at each other and both said in unison, "We Know!"

Then Liz said, "It's being delivered Thursday. That's day after tomorrow. You can wait two days, can't you?"

Deb stuck out her lower lip in a pout, "No, I can't," she moaned.

Again Stan and Liz looked at each other, nodding their heads and saying together, once more, "Yeah, we know!"

"Couldn't you deliver it sooner?" Deb begged.

"I really don't think so," Stan said. "Mr. Callan said...."

"I don't care what he said to you. I'll ask him myself." She turned sharply and hurried off toward the entrance to the dealership building.

"I'd better go head her off before she bothers him," Liz said. She bit the remaining part of the pop off and pulled the stick from her mouth. Again, not wanting to litter, she placed the sticky stick in her sweater pocket and shuffled off, barely using her cane. She was feeling pretty good today and she felt steadier on her feet lately. She always did have her good and bad days, but since the experimental treatment, she had been having more good days than usual. Whether it was actually attributable to the drug or she was just going through a period of relatively less pain and control issues, she did not know, but if it was because of the treatment, she felt irritated that the continued use of the drug had been suspended because of the mix up at the hospital.

By the time Liz caught up with her, Deb had already cornered Martin Callan in his cubicle at the rear of the showroom floor. He was gazing up at her from behind his walnut desk. There was a look of surprise and total consternation on his face.

Deb leaned over the desk, both hands flat on the polished surface and was babbling faster than the owner could process what she was saying.

"Deb!" Liz scolded, coming up behind her. "Leave the man alone. Can't you see he's busy?"

"If..if there's a problem.......?" Martin stammered.

Deb started to rant again, but Liz clamped a hand over Deb's mouth and pulled her upright away from the desk. Deb shook her off. "What are you doing?" She sputtered as she wriggled free of Liz's grasp.

"Go get in the Cherokee," Liz ordered, shoving Deb away. "I'll be right out."

Deb glared at her and stomped out.

"I'm sorry about Deb, Martin. She gets so impulsive. She's just so excited about the tractor."

Martin Callan brushed a lock of his gray streaked brown hair away from his wire glasses and back against his low forehead. He was a middle aged man; still in pretty good shape for his age, without an extra ounce of fat around his middle. He wore a blue dress shirt, open at the collar. "Yes, I know," he agreed. "Don't worry about it. No harm done." He smiled warmly, but the short brush of a mustache hid his upper lip.

"What does she want with a tractor anyways?" He asked idly.

"You know Joe had bought that extra four acres out back of our house. She has it in her head that she can grow all our own food. I told her it's more expensive to buy a tractor, but I think she just wants to play with it any how."

"Well I hope it didn't set you back too much. I felt bad, I couldn't give you a better deal on it."

"That's ok, Martin. We sold off two acres, leaving us with the four and we took out a home equity with Lew Drum at the bank downtown."

"Good. Good," he said, a hint of relieved concern in his voice. "I just don't know how you manage, is all. I know it must be hard on you with all your own medical bills and keeping Joe in a nursing home."

Liz didn't like anyone knowing her financial business. She had already said too much about the financing of the tractor, but Martin certainly had a right to know that he was going to receive his money. Still, Liz took offense. His interest was bordering on none of his business. And Liz was well aware that several residents of Mandalyn had their own ideas and suspicions where Liz's money came from. She was not about to give anyone any explanations of her business. She didn't owe any. "We manage," she clipped crisply, dismissing the topic of her finances. "Thanks Martin," she said. "We'd better be getting back home. I tire easily, you know." She started to turn away.

"I'm sorry things didn't work out for you with that experimental drug program." He said after her.

She halted and turned back toward him. A bit of a scowl was forming and Martin Callan realized what she was thinking. "Oh, Roger hasn't said anything to me about it. I assure you he keeps everything confidential about his patients. I read about the incident in the papers and I know there is trouble ahead for the hospital. And, probably for my son too. He won't talk about it to me."

"I don't know what's happening with him or the hospital," Liz said. "So far, I haven't been contacted by anyone, but I'm sure if there is to be a law suit I'll probably be called on."

"How's Joe doing these days?" Callan asked, changing the subject.

"Same as usual. Life functions work normally, but he doesn't seem to know what's going on around him. They tell me, there is still some hope of recovery, but I haven't seen any improvement in years."

"I should go see him some time," Martin said.

"I wouldn't waste my time if I were you," Liz warned. "I doubt if he'll know you. Hell, he doesn't even know me."

"But still you waste your time?"

"No. Not much anymore. I see him once a month, maybe. It's just so hard for me. I only go if I feel strong enough."

"I'm really very sorry, Liz."

"I know, Martin. You were always a good friend to Joe."

Chapter Four

"You didn't have to treat me like a child," Deb said. "After all, I am your aunt, you know. You're supposed to treat your elders with respect."

Deb had still been pouting when Liz had gotten into the Cherokee. Without waiting for Liz to settle herself and fasten her seat belt, Deb had pressed the gas pedal to the floor and sent the vehicle flying forward with a lurch and a squeal of tires. Liz had refrained from saying anything, knowing that Deb would start a conversation, when she was ready.

After the initial, lunge forward, Deb eased off on the gas and negotiated her way sensibly out of the dealership lot and turned right onto County Road 7. She had dawdled along almost at a snail's pace for half a mile; something that Deb very seldom did, unless her mind was on something else, other than getting where she wanted to go.

"I'm five years older than you, Deb," Liz said flatly.

"That makes you my Mom, does it? Huh? Then I suppose that makes you my sister, too. At last count I'm an only child. That means I don't got a sister. That means that you don't exist then."

"That's good logic," Liz said complacently.

Deb pushed the accelerator down a little more with a feeling of a little satisfaction. Liz was understanding her after all. "Just don't treat me like that in public again," Deb warned sternly. The speedometer needle shot up another fifteen miles per hour.

"O.K. Deb. Next time I'll wait until we get home."

"See that you do." She was at her usual speed of sixty miles an hour as she passed the sign saying 'Welcome To Mandalyn, Speed Limit 35 mph.'

"Deb......." Liz started to say.

"I know, I know. I'm going too fast." The horn of the oncoming truck in the other lane blared as Deb passed the car in front of her and ducked back into her lane, just in time; a split second ahead of the passing truck.

"Uh..No.. I.. uh just wondered when you were going to get around to passing that car, is all." She lied, breathing a sigh of relief and settled back in her seat as the truck sped on behind them. The truck driver held his arm out the driver's side window, his palm upward and his middle finger extended. Deb was back to normal.

Liz reached into the pocket of her sweater and pulled out another Tootsie Pop. Chocolate. Not her favorite but definitely fitting for this ride.

Deb was slowing down as she entered the center of down town, which consisted of Main Street running north and south and was about a mile long. There were a few side streets lined with centuries old shade trees and residential houses. The town was old and most of the buildings had been built in the early nineteen hundreds except for the new school, the ice cream store and pizza shop at the edge of town. A Sunoco station was a little further down the street on the opposite side and a Red and White Grocery store had been built across the street from it. They were both fairly new structures, having been built sometime during the last thirty years. Otherwise, the little village was quaint and reminiscent of earlier times. The lot was still empty from where the old movie theater had stood before it burned down almost fifty years ago, leaving the only other form of entertainment in town to drinking at the several bars and taverns that infested the town.

Deb was getting impatient, as she usually did, slogging along behind the sparse but slow traffic ahead of her. Finally she said, "Sorry I got so upset back there." She kept her voice low and said it quick, keeping her eyes straight ahead and avoiding looking at Liz. It always hurt to apologize and Deb rarely did.

Liz said nothing. She just worked at the Tootsie Pop.

The downtown business district soon gave way to a few residential houses and Deb drove past the school which had been a K through 12 school until the late 1970's, on the left, when it had then been converted to a high school. An elementary school had been built out behind it, to accommodate the increase in population, due to the insurgence of new residents along the lake to the south.

Across from the now converted high school was the town park. It was an area covering almost an acre. A large boulder near the street had a large metal plaque bolted to it, listing the names of residents who had served in World War II. No further monuments for subsequent wars had ever been established. Sitting back from the street, almost hidden by the large oak trees, shading it, stood the town hall. A battered cannon, left over from the Civil War and painted a military olive green sat in the yard, near the front entrance. The court house and the police station were housed here, in the town hall building. Two black and white police cars sat in the parking lot off to the left. A driveway led to the rear of the building as an access road to the fire department located to the rear of the town hall.

"I hate it that the tractor can't be delivered until Thursday," Deb said after awhile, and trying hard to not sound like she was griping. "I have to work Thursday." Today was her day off from her job at the 'Gossip Grill.'

"Well, you'll have it to look forward to, when you come home," Liz said.

"Yeah. But, I'm working ten until eight. Remember? It'll be dark by the time I get home. It'll be too late to play with it."

"You didn't notice, it has lights?"

"Of course, I noticed. You think I'm not that bright? Get it? Bright? Lights?"

"You amaze me, Deb," Liz quipped.

Deb smiled and picked up the speed as she passed the end of speed zone sign. The downtown district had disappeared behind them and residential buildings were becoming more plentiful.

"You'll have plenty of time to use it," Liz said. "You have more days off coming up."

"I just want to make sure we get our money's worth out of this thing."

"So do I," Liz thought to herself emphatically.

"Since when do you start worrying over spending money?" Liz said. Deb never cared about the finances; just having fun.

"I'm not. You do a good enough job of that for both of us." Deb cranked the wheel and turned right onto Clay Pool road. The Cherokee leaned sharply to the side and bounced on it springs and shock absorbers. Liz held on to the door hand rest and felt the seat belt strap strain against her.

"Well. If I didn't, we'd run out of money, and then where would we be? Hanging out at the Salvation Army and rooting through other people's garbage. That's where."

"As if you don't already do that," Deb chided. "All those garage sales, you go to. What do you call that?"

"I call that hunting for bargains. How else am I going to save money, the way you like to spend it?"

"You wouldn't catch me pawing through junk like that."

"I know," Liz said to her self under her breath. Deb hated taking Liz to garage sales. She would always try to sneak away or stay out of sight, for fear someone might see her stooping to such a low level of degradation.

Then to Deb, she said, "We haven't been to a garage sale in a long time. It must be at least four or five weeks by now."

"After I get the tractor and use it a while," Deb said. "I'll take you out and look for some." Deb had gotten her tractor and now felt obligated to toss Liz a little crumb. "It might be a few weeks off though."

"It's going to start getting colder," Liz said. "In another few weeks, we'll be into November. Next thing we know it'll be snowing and there won't be any more garage sales until spring."

"Honestly Liz, I don't know what you expect from me. I'm spread pretty thin, you know. There's only one of me."

"Thank God for that," Liz jibed. "Besides, the good Lord could never duplicate you. You're one of a kind."

"That's kind of neat, ain't it?" Deb giggled with pride.

"Yeah. Ain't it?" Liz mocked, flatly. If Deb recognized the sarcasm, she didn't show it.

"Hey look at that!" Deb exclaimed, transferring her foot from the gas to the brake pedal and shoving it hard to the floor. The Cherokee slid to an almost halt as Deb's speed went from forty five to ten miles an hour. Liz fell forward, her arms out and bracing against the dash. She felt her neck snap and pain shot down her back. She suddenly felt her so called good day ending and the start of another bad day with the monster.

"This is your lucky day," Deb shouted excitedly, without looking at Liz and seeing her face twist with pain.

"Yeah, my lucky day," Liz mumbled woefully, totally oblivious to what had grabbed Deb's attention.

The Cherokee rolled over to the side of the road and Deb brought it to a complete stop on the grassy part of the shoulder.

"It may not be a garage sale, but look. It's even better. The junk is free."

Through the passenger side window, Liz saw a pile of boxes, filled with household items. A sign taped to the center box proclaimed 'Free for the taking. Help yourself.'

"See? Do I take care of my favorite niece or do I?" Deb threw the shifting lever into park and cut the engine.

"Nobody does it better," Liz said, stretching her neck, trying to relieve the pressure. She sat silent for a few moments.

"Well what are you waiting for? Aren't you going to get out and paw through that junk?"

"I don't know, Deb. I am getting tired and I'm starting to not feel good again."

"Well don't say I didn't give you the chance," Deb said, obviously perturbed. "And don't complain if I don't get you out for a garage sale." To herself, Deb was thinking, 'this is the perfect out.' She didn't really want to take the time for Liz to look at the free items anyways, but she needed to make Liz think she was doing her a favor. Liz knew better. She always knew better.

Chapter Five

"How much longer are you gonna take?' Deb complained. Liz had left the passenger side door open after she had lowered herself carefully, with her cane to the grass. She had set the cane aside, close enough to grasp it if necessary, while she sorted through the items in the boxes. Deb had slouched down in the seat so anyone passing by, who might know her, wouldn't get a good look at her. She hoped that anyone who recognized the Cherokee, would think Liz was on her own, pawing through trash.

"Just a few more minutes," Liz answered over her shoulder. "Geez," she complained, "I've only been looking for a few minutes. Just be patient, will you?"

She hadn't found much to interest her. She had no need for the usual old books, magazines, dishes and pots and pans. So far she had set aside only a few items. One was a small pillow that she thought her dog Sissy Boom Boom could use. There was a Betty Crocker Cook Book and a photo Album and she stacked them all in a pile next to the Cherokee.

One item she found was not of interest to her, but she thought, perhaps, it was in with the give-aways by mistake. She almost dismissed it at first, thinking it was an expired insurance policy, but on closer look, she saw it was a last Will and Testament. The name on the front, said Johua P. Tilton. Liz glanced at the rural type mailbox next to the road near the driveway that led off to the Cape Cod styled house across the yard in front of her. The box had the lettering 'J. Tilton" on its sides.

"Deb," Liz called "Come here a minute. I want you to see this."

"Oh, Liz," Deb complained lazily. "I don't need to. Anything you want, just take it and let's go."

"No, I don't want it. I just want you to come here."

"Do I hafta?"

"Yes, you hafta." Liz mocked in a falsetto voice. "Now hurry on. Get out of that damn car and come here."

Deb lifted herself upright slowly, opened the door and stepped down on to the pavement. She shuffled herself around the Cherokee and came up behind Liz. "Alright, what's so all fired impor-tant?"

"Look at this." Liz shoved the paper at her.

"So?"

"So, it's someone's will."

"Big deal, it's not mine."

"Why would some one throw out a will?

"I dunno. Maybe they don't need it any more," Deb shrugged.

"Why not?"

"Who cares? Maybe they already died. Then they wouldn't need it any more."

"That's great logic, Deb. Make sure you toss mine out after I croak. Then see if you get anything of mine."

"You haven't got anything. Besides, you're not croaking for a long time yet and you don't even have a will."

"Well remind me someday, to do that. Right now I want you to take this will up to the house and give it to whoever lives there, just in case they threw it out by mistake."

"Aw, Liz. Why do I have to do it? You found it. You want to give it back. You go do it."

"Because I'm tired and that's a long driveway. I don't want to hobble that far with this cane. I'm starting to hurt and I might not be able to make it back." Then with a sugary approach to the appeal, she said, "Come on, Deb. Be a peach," Deb always liked being called a peach. "And do this for me, please. Then we can go. I'll be in the Cherokee by the time you get back."

Deb pursed her lips in defeat and took the paper. Without a word she hurried off to the front door of the house.

Liz had just seated herself in the passenger's seat, with her new found goodies beside her, when she saw Deb hurrying back. There was a tall, elderly woman with pure white hair standing in the doorway, holding the will and watching Deb jogging along the driveway. The old lady's face was narrow and wrinkled and she had a perplexed look on her face.

Without a word, Deb slid behind the wheel, cranked the engine, pushed the stick into gear and stepped on the gas. The vehicle jerked forward. Liz almost dropped the photo album, she was leafing through.

"What do you want with that?" Deb asked, glancing quickly at what Liz had.

"It's got nice pictures in it." Liz said.

"Isn't that like voyeurism?" Deb sneered. "I mean looking at someone else's private life."

"Not really," Liz said. In the rear view mirror, Liz could see the old woman at the curb, rummaging through the boxes. She picked up one of the boxes and headed back toward the house with it. Besides I'm not so much interested in family pictures as I am the pictures on the postcards. There's post cards from Jamaica and Portugal. Nice places like that."

"I still say it's all some one else's business. What they write on the postcards should be personal."

"Oh, there's nothing personal about it," Liz retorted. "Nobody says anything personal on a postcard. It's all the same old crap. 'Having a wonderful time.' Meaning, ha,ha, Look at me. I'm here and you're not. And 'Wish you were here.' Meaning, I'm glad I'm me, you slob. You deserve to be right where you are."

"You're such a cynic. You know that Liz?"

"Yeah. Ain't that great?" Liz said mimicking Deb's tone, then becoming more like herself, "Like you're not."

"Hey what's going on here?" Deb said as she turned the corner onto Beaumont Street. Houses were spread further apart here, tending to have larger lots between them and open acreage behind them. Liz and Deb lived here in the last house on the right side of the street. It was a one story ranch style much like most of the homes on the street. Next door, a crowd was gathered in front of the second house from the end. A Mandalyn police car was parked in front of the driveway, blocking it. A tall, lanky police officer, wearing a brown uniform of dark brown pants, tan shirt and a dark brown baseball cap style MPD hat, was writing notes in his pad while Marlee Drum stood at his side, her lips moving rapidly and her arms flailing about as she talked.

Deb pulled the Cherokee off to the side and parked behind the police car. Liz rolled down her window. "Hey Tom," she called. "What's going on?"

The young officer grimaced in answer. He said something to Mrs. Drum as if indicating he would be right back. He stepped up beside the Cherokee. "I can't talk now, Aunt Liz. You know that. I'm in the middle of an investigation here," Tom Hall said. "Just don't concern yourself with this. I'll talk to you later."

"But what's happening here?" Liz persisted.

"There's been a break in. But, there is absolutely nothing for you to worry about. Just go on home. You'll hear all about it later."

"But...."

"I told you, I'll see you later. OK?" Without waiting for an answer, he spun on his heel and strode back to Marlee Drum."

Liz settled back in her seat and sighed with resignation. "Take me home, Deb," she said. Her voice sounded tired with defeat.

"Just like that, Liz?" Deb said starting the engine and pulling away. "You're going to let that pip squeak of a nephew put you off like that?"

"I'm tired anyhow, Deb. I need to sleep, now. We'll find out later what's going on."

"Well as soon as I drop you off, I'm going back and find out."

"O.K. Deb. You do that."

Chapter Six

"What the hell are you doing back here, Aunt Deb? I thought I told you to go home." Tom Hall blustered as Deb burst into the living room of Marlee Drum's home.

"Don't get your shorts twisted, Tommy," Deb said with dismissal. "You told Liz to go home, not me. And nobody tells me anything, buster."

"Yeah, I know," he said with defeat. "You can stay, but just stay out of the way will you?" He went about his business, writing up his notes.

"Sure thing, kiddo." She winked at him and drifted away toward where Marlee was sitting in a green upholstered chair. Her lean face was more drawn than usual and the color in her cheeks had drained to a bland gray, matching the gray in her well coiffed hair.

"How're you doing, Marlee?" Deb said.

"I'm okay, Deb. Just a little shook. Nothing like this has ever happened before. It's just a shock, is all."

"What happened?"

"I came home from the grocery and found the house had been broken into. The back door had been jimmied and was left wide open."

"Did you see who it was?"

"No. He was already gone."

"You're lucky. If you had walked in on him, he might have hurt you."

"I suppose so."

"Did he take anything?" Deb asked.

"I don't know yet. I haven't missed anything. Anything of value, that is. But Tom's still inventorying everything."

"Does your husband know about this, yet?" Deb asked.

"Yes. Tom called him at the bank. He was out, but his secretary was going to leave him a message when he got back. He should be here soon." She fidgeted and wriggled in her chair. She quickly changed the topic of conversation and said, "How's Liz?"

"She's okay. We've had a busy morning and she got tired. I took her home so she could get a nap in."

"Deb," Tom Hall said, turning his attention away from his notes. "I thought I told you to stay out of the way."

"That's what I'm doing," she protested.

"No, no, no. I meant, you stay outside with all the other spectators."

"Well then, why didn't you say so? You've got to make yourself clear, you know. Or didn't the old man teach you that?" She was referring to

Ben MacCready, the chief of police. Ben had worked for Joe Porelli for many years and had taken Joe's place as chief after Joe became incapacitated. Deb never liked Ben MacCready. "By the way, where is the old rooster today? He usually goes out on these things."

"That's really none of your business, Aunt Deb," Tom said with annoyance.

"Tommy boy, everything is my business."

"At least, you make it so, even if it isn't."

"You got that right." Then she added, "I suppose the old boy is too busy back at the station takin' care of dispatches. If you know what I mean." She winked slyly.

"I know what you mean," Tom said. "Really, Aunt Deb, you're such a gossip and meddler." Deb had often made innuendoes that she suspected the chief of police having an affair with his secretary and dispatcher, Sadie Bell.

"Yeah, aren't I though?" She proclaimed proudly.

"Yes you are," Tom shook his head in defeat. "If you must know, the Chief had another emergency to tend to this morning. He's handling a fatal accident out on route seven, so he put me in charge of this investigation. So for now, Aunt Deb, how about getting out of here and let me do my job?"

"Sure, sonny," she said with a smile. "And tell your boss, I'm on the job."

"Whoa, whoa, there Aunt Deb," Tom said excitedly. He was afraid he knew what was coming.

"I'm going to talk to the other neighbors and start up a neighborhood watch," Deb announced. Then to Marlee, she said. "Talk to you later, honey. You take care, now." She patted her re-assuringly on the shoulder and started for the door.

"Wait a minute. Wait a minute," Tom said with annoyance. "You're not doing any such thing."

"I am too," Deb countered.

"You just leave this to us."

"Okay, okay. We will, but there's no harm in giving you a helping hand."

"Oh yes there is, if it's your helping hand."

"And what's the matter with my helping hand?" She screwed up her face and moved close to him, her hands on her narrow hips. If she had been a foot and a half taller she could have been eyeball to eyeball with him, but as it was she was still in his face with attitude.

"Well," Tom stammered a little with intimida-tion. "You know, you tend to go overboard with things. I just think it best, if you stay out of this. And that goes for Aunt Liz too."

"Well then, don't think, sonny. You might just hurt yourself."

It was almost four thirty by the time Liz arose from her nap. A nap usually meant four hours, for the monster had relegated her to a routine of four hours awake and four hours asleep on good days. This meant being up half the night and sleeping half the day. On bad days, the cycle was inter-rupted and she was lucky to sleep at all, while other days she couldn't even get up. She often said she was in the snapdragon time of her life. Part of the time she's snapped and part of the time she's draggin'.

This afternoon, Liz had awoken refreshed and ambled along the hallway toward the living room. The walls on both sides were covered with pictures of family, mostly, and a few friends. Many of the pictures were black and white and dated back to the early fifties. Liz called this her wall of Halls. She had been born Elizabeth Hall, her name having been changed to Porelli when she married.

As she entered the living room she could see the little pug, Sissy Boom- Boom still on the beige overstuffed chair in front of the TV. She still lay flat on her stomach with her neck forward and flat on the cushion before her. Her dark eyes rolled slightly to the side and her tail wagged briefly, acknowledging Liz's presence. Then her eyes rolled back to the TV screen.

When Liz had come home earlier in the day, Sissy Boom-Boom had reacted nonchalantly in much the same way for she was watching 'The Son of Lassie' on Turner Classic Movies. Now she was watching 'The Courage of Benji.'

Deb was at the kitchen table and Marlee Drum was sitting across from her. Each had a cup of coffee on the table before them. The steam had long since dissipated and the cups no longer full. "Well, look who decided to join the living," Deb chimed, looking up at Liz leaning on her quad cane.

Liz pulled on a chair and practically fell into it. "Hi, Marlee," she said, her voice a little raspy from sleep, as she settled herself and pulled her chair closer to the table. Deb had gotten up, gone to the cupboard and retrieved another cup. She placed it before Liz, then turned to the counter, lifted the coffee pot from the coffee maker and poured her a steaming brew.

"Thanks, Deb," Liz said. She sipped at the steaming cup. Hot and black, just what she needed to jump start her system. She closed her eyes and relished the hot liquid on her tongue and throat.

"So, what was going on at your place this morning?" She asked.

"Someone broke in while I was out," she said. "But they didn't take anything. I guess I was lucky. But I have to have someone come out to change the locks. Lew isn't the handy man type you know."

"He doesn't have to be. As a bank president I'm sure he makes more money than a handy man. His time is more valuable than that."

"As long as he uses his time as he should," Deb put in sharply, indicating she knew something that Liz didn't.

Liz threw Deb a look of annoyance. Marlee flushed. Deb continued. "If he spent more time at business and I mean real business, not that monkey business stuff, he'd be better off. Course it's none of my never mind, so I'm not saying one word. Not one word."

"Yeah. You're so good at that, Deb," Liz said with sarcasm. She took another sip of her coffee, looking across the cup at Marlee.

"Something going on, Marlee?" Liz asked. "I mean, besides the break in."

"Oh, I don't know," Marlee said. "It might not be anything. Just someone playing a practical joke, maybe."

"Show it to her, honey," Deb urged.

"Oh. All right," Marlee agreed, picking up the open envelope in front of her and handed it to Liz.

Liz put her cup down, took the envelope and pulled what looked like a greeting card from it. It was obviously made from a computer program. "Oh, that's cute," she said. There was a picture of a cute little poodle puppy wearing a pink bow, on it. The caption above the puppy said 'If you think she's cute...'

"Open it up," Deb urged impatiently. Marlee lowered her eyes and cringed.

'You ought to see your husband's bitch,' the caption continued on the inside. There was a picture of two scruffy dogs mating. It was unsigned. Liz's jaw dropped. She didn't say a word. She flipped the card back to the front and looked at it again, then turned it over and stuffed it back in the envelope.

"That's not a practical joke," Liz almost growled. "That's cruel." She looked up at Marlee with concern. Marlee still held her eyes downward.

"You don't think this means Lew is cheating on you?" Liz seemed to find that hard to believe. She had known Lew Drum for a long time and he had been a close friend of Joe's. Lew had always been very devoted to Marlee and he had taken very good care of her in recent years as she fought off both breast and colon cancer. She had had surgery and now had to wear a bag for body waste.

"I don't know what to think," Marlee said, facing Liz. I never would have ever doubted Lew, but lately he has seemed a bit distant. Preoccupied. But I just thought it was problems at the bank."

"Have you mentioned this to him?" Liz tapped the envelope.

"No. Of course not. I wouldn't want him to think I ever distrusted him."

"I can understand that," Liz said. Then she asked. "Just when and how did you get this?" She picked the envelope back up and saw it had no address on it, just one word, 'Marlee.'

"It was just a week ago today," Marlee said. "I always do my grocery shopping on Tuesday morning. It's not so busy, you know. It's strange," she added. "I found it on top of the fruits in one of the grocery bags when I got home and was putting the groceries away. Someone must have put it there."

"Maybe you oughtta check out the checkout girl," Deb quipped, thinking she had made a funny.

Liz cast an annoyed look at her and she quickly got the message.

"I was just trying to cheer you up a bit. I didn't mean to make light of it, you know," Deb apologized. "But, just the same, who else could have done it?"

"I don't know. But the check out girl hardly knows me. Why, I don't even know her name. I mean it's on her name plate, but I never paid much attention. Besides it's always a different clerk anyhow,"

"Were the bags ever out of your sight between there and home?" Liz asked.

"No. Only when I carried them into the house. I usually have to make three or four trips to the car. I don't remember which ones I brought in first."

"So someone could have put it in the bag while it was still in the car."

"I suppose so. But who would do that? Besides they would have to have been in the neighborhood and watching their chance."

"Have you had any trouble with anyone in the neighborhood, lately?"

"Not that I know of. But I haven't seen much of the neighbors for the last couple of years. Not since my medical problems."

Chapter Seven

"What the hell are you doing in that getup?" Liz exclaimed. She was sitting in her chair next to Sissy Boom-Boom watching television. "You look like a freakin' policeman."

Deb had walked into the living room wearing tight black pants, high top black boots, her black leather motorcycle jacket and black motorcycle helmet, with flip down sun glasses. "I'm supposed to. I'm on patrol tonight. Remember? Citizen's patrol. I told you about it. Just before Marlee left."

Marlee had left a little before five, wanting to make sure she was home when Lew finished with work. Liz had wished she could have said or done something to lift her spirits, but the way Liz was feeling, she had all she could do to lift her own spirits. She had been watching an old black and white crime movie on TCM for the last hour and a half, unable to get comfortable. The pain in her back was throbbing fiercely.

"Yeah, I remember," Liz said. "But I didn't think you'd have it organized, this soon."

"I don't mess around, you know that."

"Yeah. How many neighbors did you get to participate?"

"Just one so far," Deb tried to be evasive as she hung her flashlight on her belt.

"You mean one besides yourself?" Liz offered, skeptically. She already knew the answer.

"Well there will be," Deb answered. "Right now there's just one of us."

"You mean you're the only one."

"Well for now, yes. But when everyone sees I'm on the job. They're bound to want to help out."

"Bound to," Liz agreed. "But do you have to go out there looking like an idiot?"

"No. Of course not. That's why I dressed like this. Besides I'm patrolling on my black Honda."

"I don't know how I could have doubted you, Deb. But, what about those sunglasses? It's almost dark out there now. How are you going to see where you're going with them on?"

"Who cares? Just as long as I look cool getting there. That's all that matters."

Liz nodded, "Makes sense," she uttered.

Liz heard Deb's motorcycle go up and down the street five times before she finally drifted off to sleep. Each trip had been further apart. Deb had probably found a vantage point at each end of the street, where she could sit on her motorcycle and watch for a while before making another tour. If Liz knew Deb, she had probably found some sort of concealment to park her bike behind, just like what she thought a real policeman would do; or at least the movie and TV version of a motorcycle cop. One thing about Deb, she certainly was dedicated.

Liz's sleep was fitful for an hour before finally succumbing to the shadows of deep sleep. Sissy Boom-Boom slept quietly in her chair and silence covered the house like a shroud.

From somewhere out of the night, there was a faint stirring. A scraping sound from the sliding glass door that led out onto the backyard deck was hardly enough to arouse either Liz or Sissy. The sharp point of a knife blade slipped beneath the inside latch of the slider. The latch clicked open and the door silently slid aside very slowly, scarcely making a sound. A hand from outside, gripped the drape that covered the inside of the opening and pushed it back just enough to slip a booted foot through. A shard of moonlight and starlight from outside flashed into the kitchen and then was blotted out as a shadowy figure quickly filled the briefly opened space. The drape fell back into place as the intruder stepped all the way in.

Sissy Boom-Boom awoke to the movement and the sound of foot steps approaching. Her ears pricked up and she tilted her head from side to side. She felt a chill and her hair began to stand on end. Her skin prickled and a growl started in her throat, her eyes peering through the darkness and seeing the shadow of someone approaching. Someone who did not belong there. She jumped to her haunches and started to bark.

A strong hand reached out from the shadows and grasped her by the loose skin of the back of her neck and yanked her off the chair. Another hand clamped over her nose and snout, holding her jaws tightly shut. Sissy wiggled and twisted, trying to break free, but before she knew it the intruder had tossed her through the open sliding glass door and slammed it shut before she could retaliate.

She jumped against the door, pawing frantically and barking as loud as she could, the sound echoing up and down the street in the crispness of a cool autumn night.

Inside the house, Sissy's alarm could hardly be heard by the intruder. He moved on down the hallway toward Liz's bedroom. In the silence, he could hear her breathing evenly in deep sleep.

But, somehow, even in deep sleep, the unwanted presence permeated the darkness and drifted into Liz's unconsciousness and she began to stir. Her eyeballs began to move beneath the lids. REM, rapid eye movement which accompanied her dreams. The monster began to tug at Liz's soul and she stirred with visions of shadows, demons and monsters; shaking her out of her slumber and jolting her wide awake with the pain and terror the monster always brought on. Shards of pain shot through her entire body. Her back pained and her legs were on fire. Her arms were heavy and wooden, paralyzed and useless.

Her eyes came wide open, but they ached and even in the darkness, she knew her vision was blurred. Only vague shades of blacks and grays

loomed above her, but she knew there was movement in the darkness. A blob of black moved
from the hallway and blocking out the grey of the
bedroom doorway; a large, hulking shapeless
shadow moving slowly and quietly toward her.

Closer and closer it came. Liz tried to move,
but it was useless. With the return of the monster, she could not move a muscle. Her eyes
couldn't even open wider. She tried to scream,
but her mouth wouldn't open and her vocal
chords couldn't release a rasp or whisper. In her
brain she was screaming, though no sound was
uttered. She felt as if she would pass out, but she
couldn't physically do that. She shook with fear
from the inside, but her body couldn't even
quiver.

The dark shadow slowly took a semblance of
form as it came close to her bed. Arms were
reaching out from each side of it and reaching
toward her.

Above the silent screaming in her head, a roar-
ing clatter echoed shrilly above it. A light beam
swept momentarily through the front window in
the living room casting a brief light into the hallway behind the moving shadow. Even through
the blur of her vision, the shadow took the shape
of a large man. He whirled around at the flash
and the noise from outside. He had heard the
drone of the motorcycle, but when the light swept
through the living room and the engine ceased, he
knew someone had pulled into the driveway. He

turned and headed back down the hallway to make his escape before being found.

He was almost to the sliding glass door when the kitchen doorway to the garage swung open. The garage light flooded into the room. Deb Raymond stepped into the opening, unaware of the intruder. She had found Sissy Boom-Boom wandering in the street and had brought her home.

Sissy Boom-Boom growled and leaped from Deb's arms and flew toward the intruder. Deb fell back a step with surprise, only catching a fleeting glimpse of the shadow moving toward the sliding glass door.

Sissy Boom-Boom clamped sharp teeth into the man's thigh and swung wildly from side to side as the intruder tried to shake her off. Large hands gripped the little pug and tore her loose from him, fabric and flesh still in Sissy's teeth. He flung the little dog at Deb, striking her in the face. Sissy yelped with pain. Deb frantically tried to hang onto Sissy and hold her tight, preventing her from falling to the floor.

The intruder was gone out the back before Deb could gather her wits about her. She had only glimpsed a shadow in the dimness without getting a good look at who it was.

Quickly, she ran to Liz's bedroom, holding Sissy tightly and stroking her head lightly; the little dog trembling in her arms. She switched on the hall light as she ran, letting light filter into the bedroom rather than shocking Liz with the brilliance of a bedroom lamp.

Liz was starting to move now. She still couldn't utter a sound, but she could raise her right arm enough to indicate she was not hurt and motion toward the back of the house where the man was escaping.

Deb had seen Liz waking up with what she called the monster, many times before. She knew this was one of those times and she would be alright as soon as the effects of MS wore off. She placed Sissy Boom-Boom on the pillow next to Liz. The little pug licked her cheek, leaving traces of the intruder's blood on it.

Deb, knowing there was nothing she could do for Liz right now, whirled and ran back down the hallway, pushed aside the drape covering the open glass door and saw the man was already over a hundred yards away, running across their back lot and heading toward a stand of trees at the end of their property that ran parallel to the highway behind. He had too much of a head start on her. There was no way she could catch him on foot now.

She turned and ran through the kitchen into the garage. She had left the overhead door up. She ran to the motorcycle, jumped aboard and kicked the engine into life, at the same time turning on her headlights.

Using her feet to help guide the machine, she backed it up, twisted the handle bars, and sent it forward into the street. She took the immediate left past the side of the house onto Beauregard Street, and fed the engine gas. The motor roared loudly in the silence of the night air and wind whipped against Deb's cheeks. She worked the bars back and forth, swinging wildly in the street, trying to force her headlight beams off to the side in hopes of getting a glimpse of the running man, while still advancing forward.

At first she saw nothing out there in the open field and Deb feared that she was already too late and the man had gotten away. Then as she zig zagged again, a swath of head light flash revealed the runner. He was almost to the stand of trees. If he got in there and hid, Deb may never find him in the dark, but she guessed that he probably had a vehicle waiting for him on the other side of the trees, where Hickory Hill road ran parallel to Beaumont Street. It was an old rural back road, still gravel without the benefit of pavement or street lights. It would have been a good place to leave an escape vehicle. She turned up the gas and the Honda Rebel shot forward faster; this time taking a straight path down the middle of the street, without trying to keep the runner in sight.

In a matter of seconds she reached the intersection of Beauregard and Hickory Hill Road. She turned left, leaning into the turn, feeling the pull of the momentum and riding expertly through it. As she straightened the machine out, the beam of the headlight flooded the darkness of the back road. There was no parked vehicle there. Had she been wrong? Was the man really on foot and hiding out in the woods? She eased off on the gas and twisted the handlebars aiming her headlight to the side of the road. There was no sign of him coming out of the trees. Or had he already beaten her to the road and driven off? She whipped the front wheel of the bike back and aimed it straight forward down the road. Straining her eyes to look beyond the beam of her headlight and trying to adjust to night vision in the dark, she finally saw it. The glow of parallel red lights retreating at a high speed in the distance, winked in the darkness ahead. Tail lights! Her quarry had already taken off! Deb turned up the gas and shot forward, revving to eighty miles an hour within seconds.

The tail lights grew more visible as Deb quickly closed the distance between them. She could now make out the shape of the vehicle. It was a sedan, but it was still too dark and he was still too far ahead for Deb to discern the make and color.

The driver must have spotted her for the car's speed seemed to increase and the red tail lights receded away. Deb pushed the engine to full throttle.

The red lights, ahead, suddenly disappeared as the car topped a rise and dropped over a dip in the road. Deb followed suit and rode into the dip just as the car disappeared over the hill beyond.

With the downward momentum behind her, the Honda rolled swiftly up the ensuing hill and picked up speed as it rolled down the other side. Wind was whipping at her face even around the protective visor of her helmet and, with the speed behind her, she rolled on through an intersection without looking right or left.

She continued on for several seconds before she realized that the fleeing car was no longer ahead of her. It must have turned off at the intersection. She slowed the bike, swung to the side, did a u turn in the narrow road and rode back to the intersection.

Here, she rolled to a halt and looked both ways; left and right. There was no sign of the car. No winking red lights in the dark. There were just dark, lonely and empty country roads around her. Save for the purring of the Honda's idling engine drowning out the usual night sounds of locusts and crickets all was silent.

Chapter Eight

It was another nice day, for October. Once again the sun was shining, but the sky had a cool tinge to its blue and the billowy morning clouds carried centers of darkness that threatened of approaching cooler weather.

Deb Raymond tooled her red Honda Rebel casually down Main Street on her way to work at the "Gossip Grill". She seldom rode the black Honda around downtown Mandalyn, using it mostly on the highway for higher speeds as she had the previous night. She was dressed in her uniform of white blouse with a brown collar and matching brown slacks. She wore a black leather jacket and a red helmet which matched her bike. A decal depicting a branch with two peaches on it, was pasted to the front of the helmet. Beneath it was inscribed in italic capitals, the word 'Peaches'.

She turned the bike off the main thoroughfare and rolled into the long drive in front of the town hall, rode into the parking lot, passed a parked red Ford and a black Chevy and squeezed into a narrow space between the two police black and whites parked there.

She had deliberately set out for work early this morning so she could stop off at the police station to report the incident of the night before. Neither Deb nor Liz had felt it was necessary to report it last night. The intruder had gone and there was not much the police would have been able to do about it anyways.

When Deb had returned to the house that night, Liz was finally coming out of her funk. It was not unusual for Liz to wake up to what she called the monster and find it impossible to move or see for quite some time, but she usually came around eventually. This would usually mean a bad day for Liz, with increased pain and weakness and often blurred vision for most of the day. Some days, she would come out of it, and have a relatively good day. She could never predict from one day to the next or sometimes even hour to hour, just how the monster would dance with her. The intruder in the house had only added to her distress.

For some strange reason the monster had receded and Liz had returned to somewhat reasonable motor functions and her vision cleared to a satisfactory level. She was, however, wide awake and she knew she would remain so for several hours. She had stayed up watching TV and holding Sissy Boom-Boom in her lap, stroking the little pug gently and soothing her from the earlier ordeal. Sissy curled up snugly and slept silently, secure in the refuge of Liz's arms.

Deb had stayed up with her awhile until she was sure Liz was all right. Liz had told her to go to bed and not to worry, adding that Deb had not worried about her initially when she left her alone and went chasing the intruder in the dark.

"Aw, I knew you were okay," Deb had defended herself even knowing that Liz was just ribbing her good naturedly. "Besides, I couldn't let that bastard get away, could I?"

"Well Deb," Liz had said. "What did you think you were going to do if you had caught up with him?"

"I dunno. Never did think that far ahead."

"That's about what I figured," Liz had said.

Deb was unfastening the strap of her motorcycle helmet as she stepped into the police station. She shook her long black hair out, flinging it back and forth until it fell free. She let her eyes adjust to the dimness of the small area that served as the town's police headquarters.

Tom Hall was standing at the file cabinet in the far corner to the right and sliding a folder into its place. The drawer slammed shut and he turned just in time to see Deb tuck her helmet under her arm and start across the room toward Chief Ben MacCready's office that was separated from the rest of the room with a half height panel partition with a two foot plexiglass extension on top of it.

"Whoa, whoa, there, Aunt Deb," Tom said stepping away from the file cabinet and blocking the path Deb was obviously intent on following. "Where do you think you're going?"

"To see your boss. What do you think?"

"You can't just barge in on him like that,"

"No. Just watch me." She started forward and Tom grasped hold of her arms and restrained her.

"You know Tommy boy you better change your brand of boxers. You got your shorts twisted again."

"Aunt Deb," Tom said with a pleading tone. "What are you doing here? Don't tell me you're still meddling with what happened yesterday."

"Okay, I won't tell you that. I'll tell you something else. We had an intruder last night and he nearly scared your Aunt Liz to death."

"What...? Is she all right? Why didn't you call us right away?"

"Don't worry, Liz is okay. The guy got away. Liz was pretty shook up for a while and there was nothing you could have done then anyhow. We figured, I'd just report it this morning, so you would know about it."

"Come over to my desk, Aunt Deb," I can take the report. "There's no point in bothering Ben about it, right now."

"Just the same, Tom. I prefer to talk to Ben." She didn't sound so flippant now. "Liz would prefer it."

"Okay, but let me ask him first. Please? Just wait a minute." He turned and left her.

She turned to her left and saw Sadie Bell looking up from her desk at her. Sadie quickly returned her attention to the papers on her desk, obviously trying to ignore Deb. She was a middle aged woman who obviously still thought of herself as a hot chick, even though additional pounds and a lot of hard mileage had obviously left better days far behind her. She had a brassy red hair dye job that hardly looked natural and it was pulled up into an upsweep and pinned with a myriad of bobby pins. A curled lock fell loose onto her forehead. Her face was beginning to get puffy with the onset of age, but she had powdered it thick trying to hide the tell tale lines. Her eyes were heavily mascarade and her brows were penciled garishly. Bright red lipstick smeared full lips. Her Mandalyn Police Department uniform fitted her too tight and the blouse was opened at the neck by two buttons worth as her full figure pressed the fabric to its limits and some might say beyond. She didn't wear a bra. She used tape under her arm pits and under her breasts to push them up and out, for all to see.

"Getting a little too fat for your shirt, ain't ya, sister," Deb quipped knowing that would get Sadie's attention. She tried to stifle a mischievous smile, but her eyes couldn't hide the intent.

"Fits just right," Sadie answered, and thrust herself out even more, as if that was possible. "So, I've been told." She forced a smile.

"I'm sure," Deb agreed. She glanced toward Ben MacCready's office.

As if on cue the police chief emerged; Tom right behind him. "Deb," he gushed. "Tom said you've had some trouble. How are you? And Liz." He limped forward.

Ben MacCready was a big man. Although, just under six foot tall, he had broad shoulders and a stocky build. His middle was thick, but not really gone to fat. He had black thinning hair streaked with strands of gray, combed back over patches of bare scalp and a narrow bushy gray black mustache on his upper lip.

"We're fine," Deb answered, now ignoring Sadie who was trying to hide a glare. "And nothing was taken. Liz said I should come in and report it. What's the matter? You hurt yourself." She indicated MacCready's limp.

"Oh nothing," MacCready said. "Just bruised myself a little, sliding down the bank at an accident scene yesterday."

"Then it's just as well we didn't bother you last night. Liz said we might as well wait until morning. There's nothing you could have done then. I chased him, but he got away."

"You chased him? That was a foolish thing to do. You could have gotten hurt."

"Nah. I can take care of myself. After all, I am a duly bound officer of our neighborhood watch committee."

"Aunt Deb, you didn't go through with that crazy idea, did you?" Tom put in.

Deb scowled at him and said with annoyance, "You just heard me say so, didn't you?"

"You mean, you really got the neighbors to go for it?"

"Hey, buster. Just because you don't listen to me, don't mean other people don't." She didn't admit she was the entire watch committee.

"Really, Deb," MacCready said. "You should leave the police work to us. That's what we get paid for."

"Well, you weren't there. Now, were you?"

"No. But we would've been, if you had only called."

"It was too late by then. The perp already got away."

"Did you get a good look at him?" MacCready asked.

"It all happened so fast and it was dark. All I saw was shadows. But I could see he was a big man. He got away in a car, but I couldn't make out what kind it was."

"You did a good job, Deb. But, I would feel more comfortable if you left the police work to us. Meanwhile, I'm glad you've come to me now. I'll go out and talk to Liz a little later this morning and look around. I'll put extra patrols on your street. That might discourage our intruder and keep him away." Then he added, "Then, perhaps you can disband your citizen's committee."

"Why would I want to...." Deb started, then, noticed the consternation on the faces of both Tom Hall and Ben MacCready. She said, "If the patrol is needed again, we'll be on the job."

The police chief nodded reluctantly. "Sure." Then with dismissal, he said, "See you later Deb. It was nice talking to you, but now I've got to get back to other matters." He turned and shuffled back into his office, still favoring his right leg.

Deb looked down at Sadie Bell and said, "Looks like your boss is a little the worse for wear today."

"Don't worry. I'll take care of him," Sadie said sardonically.

Deb lifted her helmet and placed it on her head. "I'm sure you will, sweetie," Deb said with a knowing smile. She winked at Sadie, daring her to lose her cool. She fastened the strap of her helmet

"Have a nice day," Sadie said with a touch of venom in her voice. Then, noting the decal on Deb's helmet, she added, "Peaches."

Chapter Nine

All was quiet on Beaumont Street and had been ever since the gray Nissan rolled to the curb and sat parked there for almost an hour now. Traffic had been sparse with only a few cars passing by. Only two cars from the neighborhood had pulled out from driveways and had driven off and none had returned home. Watchful eyes peered through the windshield, watching the house on the corner. A woman on a red motorcycle had ridden away shortly after the car had been parked. There had been no other activity since. No one seemed to be stirring and the watcher was not sure if anyone was home. Wait a while longer, the watcher thought. Patience. Wait another car was coming down the street.

A black and white police car appeared in the rear view mirror. The watcher slumped low in the seat as the car went around and passed by. It turned into the driveway of the corner house. A big man in a policeman's uniform stepped out, slammed the car door, strode up to the front door stoop and rang the bell. He waited for a few moments, then, rang again. This time the door opened immediately as if the occupant had been almost to the door when the cop rang the second time.

A tall middle aged woman filled the doorway. She was wearing a robe and leaning on a cane. The policeman and the lady were apparently exchanging greetings. The storm door swung wide open and the officer stepped inside. The storm door and the entrance door, both, closed behind him.

"You always did make good coffee, Liz," Ben MacCready said. He was sitting at the kitchen table across from her. His cup was still steaming. "I had forgotten. Sorry I haven't seen much of you in recent years since Joe..."

"No need for apologies, Mac," Liz said. "I know I must have made you feel uncomfortable about taking over Joe's job. It was hard for me to accept it at first.

"I'm sorry about that. You've been good to Tom, letting him stay on with you. I appreciate that."

"Oh, no, no. Tom's a good man. I'm glad he stayed with me." He took a sip of his brew and said, "How is Joe, theses days?"

"Nothing's really changed much. He still doesn't know much about what's going on around him. He hasn't recognized me in years. His physical health is fine, though and the doctor's say there is a chance that he may recover one day. But I don't hold out much hope for that anymore."

"Well, here's hoping the doctors are right." He raised his cup and took a sip.

"I read about you in the paper this morning, Mac. That accident up on route seven."

Ben only nodded as he sipped his coffee. "A young woman, the paper said and you don't know who she is?" Liz continued.

"Well we can't reveal that until we notify next of kin."

"So, she wasn't from around here, then?"

Ben shook his head no, taking another sip from his coffee. It had cooled some. He took a gulp this time.

"It's a shame, though," Liz continued. "Someone so young."

"I've been reading about you in the papers too," the policeman said, lowering his cup and changing the subject. "What happened at the hospital must have been upsetting to you."

"Well, the treatments did seem to be helping me and now I can't continue them until the investigation is over." Then added as an afterthought, "Listen to me, going on about my problem," she said. "I mean, it's not that I don't feel sorry for that poor woman that died getting my drug by mistake. Oh, I guess I don't really know what I feel."

"So what is happening with the investigation?" He set his cup down on the saucer and pushed it away.

"I don't know. So far, no one's bothered me about it. But I'm sure they will. Probably when I'm not feeling well. Seems like every time something important comes up and I have to do something, whether I want to or not, this damn MS gets a hold of me and makes everything worse."

"You're not getting any better, then?" The concern in Ben's voice seemed to be genuine.

"It's not something that gets better, Mac. The best I can do is, have occasional respites from it. The drug seemed to have given me some better days, but now I'm afraid, there's no benefits left from the treatment. I was completely catatonic, last night when I saw the intruder."

"You saw, him?" MacCready said more than asking.

"Just in shadow. My vision was blurred too."

"Did you recognize him?"

"No. It was too dark and like I say, my vision wasn't good and I was so frightened."

"So you couldn't recognize him if you saw him again?"

"Sorry, Mac. No, I couldn't."

"Do you think he meant you harm? I mean, do you think he was just a burglar or do you think he had some reason to hurt you."

"Oh, I'm sure it was probably just a burglar. Especially after the break in at the Drum's yesterday morning. It was probably the same guy working the neighborhood."

Ben nodded as if in agreement. But something seemed to be bothering him. His dark eyes seemed to turn shades darker. "I don't want to alarm you, but there is a possibility that the break in at the house next door was just a mistake."

"What do you mean?"

"There was nothing taken from them and that seems odd to me. It could be the intruder meant to break into your house in the first place."

"That would have been foolish. It was broad daylight and I'm usually home at that time. If I had been home, I could have seen him. That is if I was awake. I do sleep a lot you know. Different than most people. Usually four hours awake and four hours asleep. It just happened that I was out yesterday morning.

"Besides, I haven't got anything worth stealing. The Drum's have more than I do. He'd've been better off with their house."

"That is, if robbery was the intention, in the first place," MacCready said. His face was grim and the lines around his eyes seemed to deepen.

Liz stared back at him, a bit perplexed.

"Is there any reason that anyone would want to harm you, Liz?"

Liz flushed and shook her head from side to side. "No, of course not. I'm nobody. Who would want to harm me?"

"I don't know. Maybe your relationship with Vincent Porelli."

"You still think we are part of my brother-in-law's business, don't you?" Liz was starting to get a little hostile.

"Calm down, Liz. I never said that. It's just that you are family and you did work for Michael for awhile. Maybe someone thinks you know something you shouldn't. Or, maybe there's someone harboring a grudge, who might want to send them a message. I don't know."

"Ben MacCready," Liz protested. "Vinnie never cared much about me anyways. He wouldn't care what happened to me."

"What about Michael?"

"I know you don't believe it, but Michael isn't like his father. Yes, he gets his old man out of trouble from time to time, but the majority of his law practice is totally legit. I was never involved with any cases that involved Vinnie."

"Maybe it concerns Joe," Ben's gaze was level.

"You still think Joe was involved with his brother don't you?"

"I'm not saying that. It's just that some people wonder how you afford the nursing home and your own med..."

"That's nobody's business but mine. I told you many times before where the money came from. You didn't believe me then and I guess you still don't. Maybe that's why we haven't been in touch over the years. Maybe that's why I haven't wanted to see you. Maybe it's time you should go."

"Now Liz," he said imploringly. "That's not what I meant. And I do believe you. I'm just saying, there are those who may not."

Liz said nothing. She waited for the policeman to continue.

"But I am wondering if what happened here last night actually did have something to do with Joe. Maybe somebody from the past with a grudge."

"And take it out on me? I don't think so Mac." Liz had composed herself and softened. "Joe never had any enemies."

"He had one," MacCready said flatly.

Liz's face paled more than it's usual pallor, she was remembering that day so long ago when Joe was found near death in that awful abandoned quarry. The attacker had never been found. "After all these years? Why now? Besides, whoever did it has been long gone."

"Maybe not." The policeman's tone was so low as if not really wanting Liz to hear the response.

Liz started to ask what he meant, but Ben just continued. "Is there any chance that what happened at the hospital wasn't just an accident?"

"Of course not. They simply mixed up the infusion bags. I always wondered how they kept it all straight. She got mine and I got hers. Fortunately, I only got b12 which wouldn't hurt me at all. She must have had some intolerance to the drug I was on. Besides, if it were intentional, I don't know why. I don't know anyone there. No one there would have had any reason." Then she said as an afterthought. "Is there something you know about, that I don't?"

"Of course not. I'm just asking. And I agree with you. It wouldn't make sense. I guess I've been a policeman too long. I start seeing shadows where there aren't any."

"I didn't think you had that kind of police business around here."

"Thank God," Ben said. "But I had enough of it in New York City and Buffalo before I came here. Guess I never shook my suspicious nature." He was interrupted by the phone ringing.

"Excuse me a moment, Mac." She turned and reached for a hand held phone that was sitting in its cradle on the counter. It was close enough that she didn't have to get up.

Ben started to get up, "I've got to get going any how."

Liz raised a finger, indicating she wanted him to wait. "Oh, hi Jimmy," Liz said cheerfully to the caller. She didn't even bother to cover the mouthpiece as she said to MacCready. "It's my son, Jimmy." Then to Jimmy, she said. "Just hold on a minute Jimmy, Ben MacCready is here."

"I'll let myself out, Liz," he said starting for the door. "Don't worry. We'll have extra patrols out."

She nodded, her attention to the phone. "No. No, Jimmy. Everything's fine. Yes, yes I'm okay."

MacCready glanced into the living room as he opened the front door. Sissy Boom-Boom was lying in her chair watching TV. Her eyes rolled toward the big policeman and her skin wriggled nervously. She turned her attention back to the TV when he closed the door behind him.

"I suppose it's all over town by now," Liz said.

The voice on the other end of the line said, "Well, Mom, it is hard to keep something like that a secret in a small town like this."

"Yes, I know. Especially when Deb is out there on the loose."

Chapter Ten

The door bell rang. It had been busy morning for Liz. Ben MacCready had been gone for about fifteen minutes and Liz had just finished talking to her son on the phone.

When she opened the door, she saw a young black woman standing on the stoop. She pushed the storm door part way open.

"Mrs. Porelli?" The young lady said. "Do you remember me?"

She did seem to look familiar, but Liz still had a quizzical expression on her face. Before she could think on it, the woman said, "I'm Celia Parks. I attended to you at the hospital. That day when everything went wrong."

"Oh yes," Liz's face brightened, but she was still perplexed.

"I don't mean to bother you," she said. "I've sat out front all morning, trying to get up enough nerve to come to the door. I....I need to talk to you."

"I got your address from your file. I know that wasn't right of me, but I do need your help."

Celia Parks and Liz were seated in the living room. Liz had turned off TV and Sissy had gone outdoors to the back yard. Celia had declined offers of coffee or soda.

"How about a pop?" Liz offered her the candy dish from the coffee table. She shook her head no. She had a purpose and that was all she wanted to concentrate on. "You see, I've been suspended from the hospital, because of the accident. They say it was my fault, but I was sure I checked the files and the medications when I administered them. I thought perhaps you could confirm that I did. I know I'm not supposed to be here or even talking to you, but you're the only one who can help me."

Liz unwrapped the lollipop. Grape. "I don't see how I can. I don't know what you did. I only know that you were nice and seemed competent. I just trusted that you knew what you were doing." She placed the pop in her mouth.

"There's no way I could have mixed up those infusion bags. I checked and double checked."

"Maybe someone put the wrong medicines in the wrong bags," Liz suggested.

"No," she shook her head. "Mrs. Pruitt had the bag with your name on it attached to her transom when the doctors checked it after she died. Your transom had the bag with her name on it."

"I did go to sleep for awhile, maybe someone switched them, then."

Again Celia shook her head. "No one saw anything like that happen. Besides who would do that? Why?"

"Seems to me, honey, that you're doing a pretty good job of convincing me you screwed up."

"If I wasn't so sure that I checked the bags, I probably would think so too. I..I just don't know what to do. The hospital is in big trouble over this and they need someone to take the blame. I guess that's me. I just can't be fired over this. I'll never be able to work in a hospital again. I just don't know what to do. I'm sorry I came here and bothered you. I..I just thought... Oh, I don't know what I thought."

"Well it seems to me, dearie, that what you need is a good lawyer."

"I wouldn't know who to go to. Besides I don't have money to pay a lawyer."

"Maybe you don't have to, sweetie." Liz smiled. "Maybe I can help you after all."

Vincent Motors was a sprawling dealership with several acres of new and used cars for sale. It was one of the largest if not the largest in the Buffalo area and was very close to the mall in Depew.

Celia Parks turned her gray Nissan off the main thorough fare and drove up close to the building near the rear entrance. The parking spot said 'reserved for staff and personnel'. Liz assured Celia that it was all right to park there. She drove nose first into it and turned off the engine.

Vincent Motors was owned and operated by Liz's brother-in-law, Vinnie Porelli. Vinnie thought the name Vincent was more respectable and drew attention away from being Italian owned and possibly mob connected, even though everyone knew he was the owner and already had their opinions about him. How could anyone help but not know about him. Vinnie insisted on doing his own commercials, using the tired cliche'd method of standing out in front of his dealership, holding up huge signs, indicating the fabulous deals he offered. He would shout at the top of his lungs as if by sheer volume he could coerce the public to come driving into his dealership by the droves, to drive away with the best deal in town.

Liz hated seeing those commercials on TV. She always thought Vinnie looked like a huge, overgrown penguin. His fat round head sat on the top of his shoulders, flab around his neck hid any semblance of a neck at all. His rotund body flared around the middle and it was a wonder that the belt he wore was even big enough to go around, much less hold his pants up. One would never know, by looking at them, that Vinnie and Joe were brothers. Vinnie looked like a slob and Joe was always trim and fit, and looked like a gentleman.

"That's Michael's car over there." Liz pointed to the silver Lexus parked three spaces down.

Liz had called her nephew, Michael Porelli, to see if he could help out Celia. He had told Liz that he wouldn't be in his downtown Buffalo office that afternoon, but he would be out at his father's dealership. Depew would be a shorter ride for Liz. He could meet them there.

Celia had offered to drive and bring Liz back after the meeting. They had climbed into Celia's gray Nissan and pulled away from the curb without noticing the black 1996 Chevy parked further down the street behind them. Its driver started the engine and drove forward following the two ladies at an unnoticeable distance.

Liz and Celia entered through the rear door and Liz led the way   down a narrow hallway toward the front of the building, where Michael used an office when he was there.

He was sitting behind the desk and Vinnie was standing over his shoulder looking at a file that was on the desk in front of Michael. They both looked up as Liz framed herself in the doorway.

"Liz?' Vinnie said with surprise. Then to Michael as if Liz wasn't there, "What the hell's she doing here, Mike?"

"Well, hello and how are you too, Vinnie," Liz said and stepped into the office; Celia at her heels.

It was crowded now in the small office.

"Hello, Liz," Michael said pleasantly with a smile and ignoring his father. He never called her aunt, since she had worked with him for a few years as a paralegal. "How are you? It's good to see you again." He pushed his chair back and arose to his feet, pushing Vinnie aside, as if he weren't there. Michael was a young man of medium height and slight build. He wore brown plastic rimmed glasses that matched his dark brown hair. He took more after his mother, Constance, who was petite and light complected. Michael's brother, Francis, on the other hand, was built a little more like his father, tending to be heavy set, but not as large as Vinnie and in no way did he look so grotesque. In temperament and personality, Francis was more like his mother and not at all like Vinnie. Francis had chosen not to follow his father's footsteps in the family business. He had instead opted for the priesthood.

Vinnie half stumbled backward into the corner. "Hey watch it, sonny," he complained.

"We were just finishing up, Liz. You're right on time." He pushed the file toward his father in dismissal.

"What? You knew she was coming?" He blustered.

Mike practically pushed him around the desk toward the door. Vinnie brushed against the two ladies as he squeezed by. "We'll talk about it later, Dad," He closed the door on his father, leaving him standing in the hallway fuming to himself.

"Your father hasn't changed any," Liz said with a chuckle.

"Only for the worst," Mike answered.

"Mike, this is my friend Celia that I spoke to you about on the phone."

"Hello, Celia. Please sit down."

Celia smiled slightly. Mike had a way about him that made people feel comfortable.

"How's your mother?" Liz asked as the two ladies seated themselves"

"Mom's fine. She's out of town for the next two weeks with her sister."

"She probably needs a getaway from your father."

"I'm sure she does, but this isn't exactly a pleasure trip. Her sister is very ill. Cancer. Nasty business that cancer."

"I'm so sorry to hear that," Liz said. She was genuinely sorry about the woman with cancer, but as far as Michael's mother was concerned, there was never any love lost between them.

Constance, as was her name, had always felt she was better than anyone else. She never liked Liz, in particular, because Liz could always take something cheap and make it look expensive. Constance had it all; nothing but the best, but no matter how expensive it was, she always made it look cheap. They had known each other since high school. Constance was popular with the boys and was known as a beneath the bleachers girl. Then as she grew up, she had affair after affair. When she had tried to seduce Liz's own beloved Joe, Liz could no longer tolerate her. From then on, Constance would always look at Liz with a face that was so mean and ugly and then turn and run. Liz often said that if she could sue Constance for face and run, she would win that case hands down.

"I use to see Frank whenever I felt like going to church." Liz changed the subject, choosing not to dwell on Michael's mother any more. "But since he took over that parish in Buffalo, I haven't seen much of him."

"He doesn't seem to like it as well as he did when he had the parish in Mandalyn. The Buffalo parish is just too big for him." Michael commented, then asked, "How's Deb?"

"Still Deb, I'm afraid," Liz said. Mike could fully understand that.

Michael took a yellow lined note tablet from his left hand top drawer and placed it on his desk, getting right to the business at hand. He asked Celia for her name, address and phone number and wrote them on the pad.

"You told me a little bit about the problem on the phone. Perhaps you could run it by me again."

Liz took three tootsie pops from her pocket and held them out in front of her. "How about a pop?" She said.

Celia and Mike both declined. She put two back in her pocket, keeping the orange out. She unwrapped it as she explained about her participation in the experimental drug program at the hospital and how the infusion bags had gotten mixed up, resulting in a fatal accident to another patient.

Celia explained how she had administered the drugs and the actual procedures involved.

"Do you know the name of the woman that died?" He asked Celia.

"Yes. Her name was Jane Pruit. I have a clipping of the newspaper article, the day after it happened." She fumbled in her purse and pulled out a folded piece of newsprint. She unfolded it and smoothed it out on the desk before her.

Mike looked at it and read, "Jane Pruitt, aged 57." Read some more to himself. "It says she resided in Amherst with her husband, Arnold Pruitt, president of Amalgamated Concrete Delivery in Buffalo." He wrote down the names and addresses on his pad. "Two grown children," he continued. "Both married and moved away. She was being treated for vitamin B12 deficiency. This was just one of several treatments she had received over the last year. Her physician was Hubert Tombragle. Maintains an office, also in Amherst, and on staff at Amity Hospital."

"You attended to Mrs. Pruitt, before?" Mike asked.

"Once, about a month ago. I'm not always on duty when she's in."

"What kind of a patient was she? I mean, was she difficult or pleasant?"

"Oh I don't know. She was a bit snooty, I think. Didn't respond to small talk. I got the feeling that she felt she was slumming when she came into the hospital. She was obviously a woman of means."

"I see," Mike mused to himself. He was silent for a moment, thinking.

"Who else was there in the infusion room at the time?"

"Well there was the RN who oversaw the treatment, and another attendant, like myself."

"No one else?"

"No, not that I remember ."

"Think. Administrative assistants, physicians, orderlies."

"Yes there were two women in the office. Oh, and a janitor came through picking up the trash, but none of them had anything to do with the patients."

"Do you know any of their names?"

Celia shook her head, "No, only the other attendant. Shirley Robbins." To Liz she said, "She's the one that messed up your needle, Remember?"

Liz nodded, still working on her pop.

"What about the RN?"

"Her name tag said N. Taylor, but I don't know what the N stands for. I would guess Nancy. I've seen her there several times, though. She's not very friendly."

"Did any of them pay any particular attention to the Pruitt woman?"

"I didn't notice anything out of the ordinary."

"How about, the other patients? Did they have any interaction with her?"

"None that I could see. As I said, Mrs. Pruitt seemed quite aloof."

Mike nodded. He thought about things for a minute or so, then, wrote some notes on his pad. When he finished, he looked up and leveled his gaze at Liz. She was unwrapping another pop.

"You know Liz, that if I take on Celia's case, I won't be able to represent you, if you are called into the hospital's investigation and I'm sure you will be."

"So far, I haven't heard anything from anyone."

"They will. It might take some time. But they will. Have you discussed this with your doctor?"

"I saw him last Thursday. He didn't say much about the hospital, though. Mostly he was concerned about how I was feeling and what I thought of the drug as far as I used it."

"Roger Callan is your Doctor, isn't he?"

Liz nodded. "He's my doctor here, but he had referred me to Doctor Blakeney at Amity. He was in charge of the drug program."

"Actually, he's in charge of the infusion area, also." Celia said.

"So Mrs. Pruitt would have had to consult with him, just as Liz had," Mike said, more as a question.

"Oh, I'm sure," Celia said. "So would all the other patients that were there for treatment."

Mike thought about that for a second, then said, "I'll contact Roger, first. I've known him a long time." Then to Celia, "In the meantime, we won't set up anything formal as far as representation until I look into things a bit. I want to be able to choose which side of the fence, if need to. Whether I need to be representing Liz or you, I don't know. But, I'm telling you this. I will help you."

Chapter Eleven

"Aren't you going out on patrol, tonight, Deb?" Deb wasn't in her get up for street patrol. She was sitting in her chair in the living room and leafing through the album that Liz had picked up the day before.

It was nine o'clock and Liz was just getting up from her nap. She had been tired from her trip to Depew. Liz and Celia had returned about four thirty. Celia dropped her off and then drove off to her home in Buffalo. Neither lady had noticed the black Chevy that had waited near the entrance to Vinnie's dealership and followed them back to Mandalyn. Once again it had parked down the street and waited while Liz got out and went into her house. When Celia Parks drove off again, the black Chevy had continued to follow her.

"No. Not tonight, Liz. I'm gonna stay right here in case that dude tries to come back. If he does he won't get away with just a little bite from a pug dogie. Poor, Sissy," Deb said putting down the album and picking up the pooch from her chair, and stroking her. "Bet that man tasted real bad. Huh, little baby?" She scratched her behind the ears.

"I doubt he'll try it again," Liz said. She sat down in her chair. "Besides, Mac said he'd have extra patrols on."

"So, it's back to 'Mac' again, is it? What happened to 'pig' and 'Yosemite Sam' and 'Deputy Dawg'? He came over here and schmoozed his way into good graces again?"

"Nobody schmoozes me," Liz said. "It's just that it's been a long time since he took Joe's job. I can't hold a grudge forever."

"Why not? I do it all the time."

"Yeah. I know."

"Just you be careful, dearie," Deb said. "I wouldn't trust that weasel any farther than I can throw a bull."

"Seems to me you throw that all the time. Pretty far too."

"See. I fed you a straight line. You took it just like I thought. I knew you'd say that."

"Well, I'm glad I didn't disappoint you." Liz added, "I think you're being unduly harsh on him. I don't think he's as bad as you make him out to be. I certainly don't see him as a weasel."

"Well, I do," Deb came back sharply. "Him messing around with that slut, Sadie Bell. A married man at that. I wonder if his wife knows about it."

"How do you know, he's actually cheating on her?"

"Hell, he's in the same room with Sadie all day. No way is she gonna let him alone."

"Well, I'm sure Mac would have something to say about that, though."

"Sure he does," Deb said. "That's what I've been trying to tell you. He says 'yes' and you better believe it."

"Deb, you have such an evil mind."

"Thank goodness, one of us around here has sense," Deb said. "Mark my words, that Ben MacCready is no one to trust. And Sadie's not the only woman he runs around with, either. I tell you, that man is a womanizer, if I ever saw one." She had that knowing smile on her face like she knew something she was just dying to tell.

"Alright, Deb," Liz conceded. "Let's have it. Just what is it you think you know?"

Deb giggled, put Sissy down on her own chair, picked the photo album back up and flipped through several pages. "Here it is," she said triumphantly. Her eyes sparkled with glee as she twisted the book around and held it up toward Liz. "Am I right or am I wrong?"

Liz hobbled forward on her cane, leaned forward, bending at the waist, and peered at the page. There were three pictures on the page. The top row had two wallet size snapshots of a boy about seven years old and a blond haired little girl of four or five. The bottom half of the page consisted of a 5X7 shot of two elderly couples sitting at a table in a plush restaurant. They were huddled together posing for the shot. All of the photos were in color.

"What?" Liz muttered, unable to see anything of special interest. "Somebody's memories. I thought you were against this sort of voyeurism."

"Never mind the high faluting words. Look close and tell me what you see in that bottom picture."

Liz leaned closer and squinted. "Four old farts out drinking and having a good time."

"No. No. Look in the background. The second table behind them. Off to the right. In the corner. Isn't that your good friend Mac, the Chief of Police."

Liz set her cane aside, took the album from Deb and drew it close. After a moment, she said, "It does look like him. I'm used to seeing him in uniform, though. He looks different in a suit and tie."

Deb waited expectantly.

"But, I guess you're right. It is him," Liz admitted.

"And who's that broad next to him? Looks pretty cozy to me." She double hiked her brows in a huba, huba fashion. "She looks half his age. The old fart should be ashamed of himself."

Liz carried the album over to her chair and sat down. "I wonder where this was taken and when," Liz mused more to herself than to Deb."

"More to the point," Deb said. "Who's the young chick?"

Liz pulled the picture from the page and turned it around. The date on the back was just three months ago. "This was taken recently," Liz said. "The restaurant doesn't look familiar. Certainly no place in Mandalyn. Probably Buffalo. Hey wait a minute. She look's familiar. Now where have I seen her before?"

After a moment of thought, she said, "You know what? She looks like one of the attendants at the hospital. You know, when I went for the infusion. Oh, that couldn't be." She closed the album, placed it on the end table next to her chair and slapped the photo down on top of the album cover. She plucked a pop from the candy dish and unwrapped it. Lemon. "It's none of our business, anyhow," Liz said.

"Everything's my business," Deb reminded her.

"Yeah, I know."

The phone rang and Liz picked up the hand held from its cradle on the end table. "Hello. Oh hi, Celia. You got home okay?"

"Yes, but something is bothering me. I didn't want to bother you again, but after I thought about it, I decided I should tell you about it," Celia said from the other end of the line.

"You're not bothering me," Liz said. "You can call me anytime. What's up?"

"It might be just my imagination and I might just be jumping at shadows." There was a tremor in her voice.

"What?"

"When we went to Depew today, did you happen to notice a black car parked down the street?"

"No. Can't say as I did. Why?"

"Well when I got home and looked out my window, I noticed a black car parked on the street outside my apartment building. There was a big man sitting behind the wheel as if waiting for someone. At first I didn't think anything of it, but later when I was getting ready for bed, I went to the window to draw the drapes, and I saw the car was still there. The man was still in the car.

"It was dark and he could probably see me in the window with the lights on behind me, because as soon as he saw me there, he started the car and drove off fast."

"It just may be one of those things," Liz said trying to be reassuring. "Coincidence, I mean. Besides, why would someone be watching you?"

"I don't know," Celia said. "Maybe, I'm being investigated because of the hospital thing. Maybe, they hired a private investigator or something."

"Oh, private eyes are TV stuff," Liz scoffed. "I don't think that really happens in real life. Maybe you're just getting yourself worked up about nothing."

"I hope you're right," Celia said. "I said before that I might just be jumping at shadows, but the more I thought about it, the more I seemed to remember that same black car or one like it, parked on your street as we were leaving today. Then when we left your brother-in-law's dealership, I thought I saw it again. I didn't think too much of it at the time. There are a lot of black cars on the road. They all pretty much look the same.

"I'm sorry I bothered you about this, Liz. I guess I've just got too much imagination for my own good."

"No. No bother. Call me anytime. If it will make you feel better, maybe you should report it to the police."

"No. No. Not with all the trouble with the hospital. I just don't want anymore problems."

"Maybe you should call Michael," Liz suggested.

"No. No. I probably am just making too much out of this. But if I have anymore trouble, I will call him."

"Well, call me too. Will you?"

"Sure Liz and thanks a bunch." She hung up.

Chapter Twelve

The tractor was delivered early in the morning. Liz had been up awhile and had seen Deb go off to work on her red Honda as usual. She had been gone only a few minutes, before the flat bed truck carrying the tractor arrived. It was a good thing, for if they had come before Deb left, she may not have gone to work after all. It would have been too much of a temptation for her to stay home.

Liz stood outside on the front stoop while the truck backed into the gravel driveway that led to the two story barn shaped Duro Shed, on the far side of the house. Deb had left the doors open for the tractor to be parked inside.

Two men got out of the cab and Liz was surprised that Martin Callan, himself had accompanied the driver for this delivery. He waved to Liz and walked across the yard to meet her, while the driver lowered a ramp from the rear of the flat bed and proceeded to release the chains that held the tractor in place.

"You deliver now, do you Martin?"

"Not usually," He said as he stepped up to her. He had a clip board in his hand. "It's such a nice day. We're not going to have many more of them." He looked up at the sun, already halfway to the apex of the clear blue sky. "Thought, I'd like to get out of the office for awhile."

The tractor engine started as the driver, now mounted on the seat of the tractor started to back the machine out of the truck bed and onto the ramp.

"I just need to get your signature on this delivery receipt, if you don't mind," Martin said, handing Liz the clip board. There was a pen tied to it with a string.

Liz took it and looked at the document.

"Just sign at the bottom where the X is," Martin said.

"Good morning, Liz." A man's voice sounded from next door. Liz looked up as she finished signing. She saw Lew Drum coming from his house toward his car. He was dressed up as usual with dark suit and tie. He carried a thick satchel like brief case. She waved, "Morning, Lew."

Lew Drum was a big man and the suit made him look even bigger. The suit coat tended to hide the bulging pot of a belly that protruded over his belt and sagged. He had a thick head of black hair, flecked with streaks of gray, but overall he was an impressive good looking man for his age.

"So, that's the new tractor, you were buying," he said. "Nice." Then as he saw Martin turn and look in his direction, he said, "Martin? Is that you?"

"How are you doing, Lew?" Callan shouted back as he took the clipboard back from Liz, and waved it in the air as a friendly salutation. Then he said "Good to see you. Got a minute?"

"Sure," Lew answered, motioning him to come on over.

"Thanks, Liz," Martin said starting to turn away. "If you don't mind, I'd like to talk to Lew for a moment." He smiled broadly. "My man will leave the keys to the tractor in the ignition and close up the barn for you. Okay? I hope you enjoy the tractor."

He hurried across the yard into the Drum driveway.

Liz watched as the tractor rolled down the ramp into the driveway and continued on toward the barn. As it passed by the side of the house and she could no longer see it, she glanced back toward the Drum's place. Martin and Lew were having a discussion of some sort and it didn't look like casual small talk. Both men were quite animated with arms and hands flailing about with emphasis. Neither man had a friendly expression on his face.

"I wonder what that's all about," Liz thought to herself as she fished a lollipop from her sweater pocket and unwrapped it. Lime.

The discussion ended and Lew Drum hurriedly got into his car, started the engine and backed out of the driveway. Martin Callan stomped across the yard, passed Liz without looking at her and got in the truck. The driver had already finished putting the tractor away and was waiting in the cab. The engine roared into life and the big vehicle lumbered out into the street, straightened out and headed off down the road.

Liz watched until the truck disappeared around the corner at the end of the street. She turned to go inside. She was suddenly feeling a chill that she had not felt earlier. A numbness started to seep into her leg muscles. "The weather's about to change," she thought. Today may be starting out to be one of those days that she would have to host the monster.

The light was flashing on her phone answering system when she got back inside the house. She pushed the button and the voice came on saying "You have one new message." She pressed the listen button and a man's voice came on.

"Liz. This is Roger. Please call my office as soon as possible and make an appointment. I have something important to discuss with you." He left his number. Liz already knew it by rote.

Liz quickly picked up the phone and dialed. Doctor Callan's receptionist came on and Liz told her she was returning the doctor's call. The receptionist said there was an opening at one o'clock this afternoon and could she make it. Liz agreed and hung up.

She would need to get nap in and she would have just enough time for a short one. With Deb at work she would then drive the Cherokee herself. She just hoped she would be up to the task when she got up, if she had to,

She started to shuffle off to her bedroom, then thought of something. She went back to the phone, took it from its cradle and punched in a number. It rang at the other end four times before a young female voice came on.

"Hello, Jennifer?" Liz said as she recognized her niece's voice.

"Oh, hello Aunt Liz." She had recognized Liz's voice immediately, also. "But have you forgotten, I'm not Jennifer any more? I'm Daisy Mae now."

"Oh, yes. Of course. How silly of me to forget. I'm sorry."

"That's okay. Mom and Dad keep doing that all the time."

"Well, I'll remind them when I see them," Liz said. "Is your Dad there?"

"Yeah, sure. You want to talk to him?"

"Yes."

"I'll go get him. Nice talking to you, Aunt Liz."

Liz could hear the girl setting the phone down and heard her shouting in the background. "Dad. It's for or you."

"Nice talking to you too, Daisy Mae," Liz said to herself as if the girl was still there

After a few moments, a man's voice came on the line. "Hi, Liz. How're you doing? Tom told me you had a little trouble out there, the other night. I've been meaning to call, but with football season and all, I hadn't got around to it?"

Hal Hall was Liz's brother and Tom Hall's dad. He had retired from the Mandalyn High School, where he had taught Chemistry for the last thirty years. In addition to his teaching duties, Hal had also coached the high school football team. This was a job he continued on a contract basis after retirement and the season was now in full swing. The boys had always thought a lot of Hal and because of the sound of his name, "Hal Hall" and his grittiness on the football field, his name had become slurred as "Hell Hole." The name was aptly suited for him, although he was a diminutive looking man of slight build and narrow shoulders. The top of his head was completely bald with a wraith of hair along the back of his head between his ears. He let several strands grow long and he tied it in a sort of spindly pony tail.

"Hal," Liz said getting right to the point. "Would you be able to take me to the Doctor's today. I need to be there at one. So I would need you to pick me up at noon."

"Sure, Liz. Have you got a problem.?"

"I'm not sure, yet. I'll tell you later."

Hal Hall rolled his canary yellow Volkswagon up to the curb in front of the Tilton residence. The piles of boxes containing free stuff were practically empty now and there was litter all around the half strewn boxes.

Liz had purposely asked Hal to pick her up early enough so they could stop off at the house where Liz had picked up the photo album two days before. She had not yet had time to explain to Hal what was going on.

Hal was already out of the car and over on Liz's side by the time she eased herself out of the seat and propped herself up on her cane. She was standing shakily and her legs were aching with pain. This was turning out to be a real bad day. Nonetheless, she held the album tight under her free arm while she trudged forward on the long driveway to the house. Just two days ago, when she was feeling much better, she had sent Deb up the walk for her. Today, she was determined to do it herself.

The same woman came to the door that had greeted Deb on Tuesday. She held the screen door open only part way as if not sure she should be opening it to strangers.

"Hi," Liz said with a smile. "I was here the other day and picked up this photo album from along side the road and I was wonder............"

"So that's where it went," the old lady interrupted her and pushed the door open wider, practically pushing Liz backward into Hal, who was standing a pace behind her. She whipped the album out of Liz's hand, pulled it inside the door and was letting the door swing shut, when Liz shot her free hand forward and gripped the edge of the door, holding it open.

"I just want to ask you a question about one of the pictures," she blurted quickly before the old woman went away.

"You should be ashamed of yourself going through other people's personal memories." She snapped the door shut with a clang, as Liz released her grip and pulled her fingers away just in time to avoid getting them pinched. She felt the metal brush her fingertips.

Liz rubbed her fingers together and said dejectedly, almost to herself, "That's what Deb said too." She turned slowly and started back toward the car. God! What a long driveway, she thought.

Hal had just driven them away, when another car approached, slowing down; its engine almost idling. The black Chevy rolled up to the curb and stopped.

The engine died and the door opened. A shiny black boot emerged from the car and was placed firmly against the pavement.

Chapter Thirteen

"I don't seem to be feeling any affects from the treatment any more," Liz said. She was sitting on the edge of the examining table in Doctor Roger Callan's office. "I'm starting to have more bad days again."

"I'm sorry things worked out the way they did, Liz," Roger said. He was a medium framed man in his mid thirties. His light brown hair was parted almost in the middle, but just a little to the left side. It hung full around his ears and a lock curled on his forehead.

"Maybe, once things are straightened out, we can try again. I really don't think the drug is dangerous. I think when we find out what really happened to the Pruitt woman, we'll find that the drug wasn't really at fault."

"What do you think the problem was?" Liz asked.

"I don't know. She must have had some other condition that couldn't handle the drug."

"Has the hospital been in touch with you about it?" Liz asked.

Callan looked into her face, seeming to struggle with the question.

"Of course," Liz said, seeing his uneasiness. "You don't need to answer that. I probably shouldn't have asked. What with all this privacy stuff and all."

"Oh, no. That's quite all right. You have every right to know. Besides, I've already talked to Michael about it. He said you were concerned that you might be involved in an investigation. And that's really what I wanted to talk to you about."

"I was afraid of that."

"Don't worry about it though. Nothing was your fault but you may be called to testify. I don't think you need a lawyer and I told Michael that. I'm sure we can work things out together ourselves.

"The brunt of the investigation will be on myself, Doctor Blakeney and the hospital chief of staff, as well as the pharmaceutical company. These types of things tend to take a long time to straighten out. Sometimes, years.

"You may be called on from time to time, but I don't think you'll be involved for any prolonged period of time in each instance. The real bad news is we can't continue with the experimental drug, until this is cleared up. For now, we need to try something else to help you get by."

"Haven't you already tried everything?" Liz asked.

"As long as science keeps working on this thing, we'll never have tried everything. But for now I'm going to try something else on you for a couple of weeks."

He went to a cabinet, opened a drawer and took out an envelope designed for dispensing tablets. "These are samples," he said. He wrote in pencil on the envelope. "Take one tablet four times a day before sleeping."

"Let's try these and see how they work. If they help, I'll write out a prescription and put you on them for an extended period. Fair enough?"

"Fair enough," Liz agreed.

Liz slept fitfully. She tossed and turned, unable to get comfortable, even when she rolled over onto her stomach, which was her preferred position. Although not quite awake and not quite asleep, she still felt pain with every movement. Flashes of images and a crackle of sounds flickered in her brain; many so fleeting that she couldn't grasp them and this distressed her even in her twilight state.

She began to writhe in the bed and started to breath heavily, as if she were living through some awful ordeal in an alternate universe buried somewhere in her sub consciousness. Her head began to ache and loud sounds filled her ears and made them hurt. Shadows rolled in beneath her eyelids as they slowly opened to slits. The noise in her ears grew louder and louder. Suddenly she jerked wide awake, rolled over on her back and sat up abruptly, clutching the blanket to her chin. Her mouth opened wide and she screamed with no sound. Her heart pounded in her head and sweat beaded on her brow. She was like a little girl awakening from a bad dream filled with terror.

Then as quickly as she had awoken, she realized what had happened. She slumped back against her pillow and relaxed. Her breathing slowed and her heartbeat began to subside.

She glanced toward her bedroom window and could see lights moving outside in the dark. The noise had continued, but reverberated in a normal level. As she came fully awake now, she realized the sound was the clatter of the tractor engine.

Liz smiled, even though a bit ashamed of herself for her night terror. She now realized that Deb must be home from work and couldn't resist trying the tractor out before going to bed. She lay back and rested a bit, listening to the drone of the machinery as Deb drove it all over the back lot. Occasionally, she would see beams of light flash past the window. Deb's presence was somehow reassuring and Liz couldn't remember when she finally drifted off to sleep with the drone of the tractor still in her ears.

Chapter Fourteen

The black and white police car turned the corner onto Beaumont Street. There were no street lights here and most of the houses were dark. Tom Hall peered into the darkness before him; his head swinging from side to side, looking into the yards of the houses on both sides of the street.

All was quiet, this night and without the light of a moon, the street was extremely dark and lonely. He had cruised half the length of the street when he thought he saw movement in the shadows of a large bush in the yard of the third house from the end of the street on the left.

He slowed the black and white, turning on his spotlight and shining it toward the bush. Nothing, but shadow at first then the tiniest of movement was detected. Could be the wind. He rolled down his window and felt no breeze. He looked at the branches of other trees on the street. They were motionless.

He moved the spotlight back and forth, up and down, examining the bush closer. A shoe protruded from behind the bush. Someone was standing there behind it.

Hall left the engine running and opened the car door. He was reaching for his billy club that lay on the seat beside him as he stepped out. His foot was barely on the pavement when whoever was behind the bush darted out from cover and started running toward the backyard.

"Stop!" The officer shouted as he leaped into a run, leaving the car door open. He was across the street in two strides and followed the runner across the dew wet grass. There was a sharp chill in the air and Tom sucked it into his lungs as he plunged forward.

He could barely see a moving shadow against the blackness of night, but he could hear the runner breathing heavily. "Stop!" Tom shouted again as he ran. "Police! Stop!"

The shadow almost stopped, stumbling forward as if trying to make up his mind, to stop or keep running. Apparently, he decided against giving himself up, for he twisted and ran off to the right into the yard next door. His hesitation gave Tom an edge and the policeman closed the distance behind him to just a few strides.

The runner was in Liz's back yard now, with only Beauford Street in front of him. He turned quickly to the left and started to run across the open lot out back, when he heard the drone of Deb's tractor. He froze instantly as the headlights of the machine bathed him in bright light.

Wild eyed at the sight of someone before her, Deb slammed on the brake. The wheels locked and the rubber tires slid across the wet grass, coming to a halt only a few feet from the runner, as another body came hurtling out of the darkness in a flying leap. Tom Hall's arms wrapped around the man's shoulders and shoved him vigorously to the ground.

The two figures rolled in the wet grass, momentarily, until the police officer managed to gain the advantage and rise first holding the other man flat on his face in the grass. Hall pulled the man's arms behind him and snapped handcuffs on his wrists.

Deb cut the engine and watched with wonder.

"Where's your uniform? Aren't you going to work?" Liz asked as she came from the hallway into the kitchen.

Deb shook her head. She had that sly smile on her face she usually had when she was dying to tell something.

"Don't tell me you're staying home to play with that damn tractor. Didn't you get enough of it last night? You damn near kept me awake all night," she lied.

"Nope, I ain't doin' that neither." She giggled mischievously. "Have I got something to tell you."

"Well, get it over with, before you bust a gut." Liz lowered herself into a chair at the kitchen table.

"We caught him. We caught the burglar." Deb beamed with pride.

"What to you mean? You caught him?" She was still trying to make sense of it through the haze of her half awake mind. "Who? Who's we?"

"Why, Tom and me of course. We caught him outside in the back lot last night. I ran him down with the tractor."

"You ran him down? You didn't...."

"Nah, I didn't hurt him, none. I just stopped him so Tom could arrest him."

"What was Tom doing here?" She absentmindedly reached for the candy dish and took out a pop and unwrapped it. A little early for it, but what the hell.

"He was on patrol and spotted him lurking about the neighborhood." Then she added, "I was on patrol too."

"With the tractor?"

"Of course."

"I thought you were just playing with it."

"I never play, dearie."

"Yeah. Sure." Liz put the pop in her mouth. Lime. She hated lime first thing in the morning.

"So you still haven't told me why you're not going to work," Liz said after a moment.

"Because we have a date at the police station. You and I." Deb said proudly.

"What for? Why do I have to go?"

"So you can identify him of course."

"I couldn't identify anyone. I told you it was dark and I couldn't see well. My eyes were all out of focus, just like they are today. I'm afraid today is going to be even worse than yesterday. And that wasn't good. I called Hal yesterday and had him drive me to the doctor's."

Deb's face darkened and she became much more serious. "Oh, I'm sorry. I didn't know. I'm sorry I kept you awake last night, too."

"Don't worry. You didn't."

"You mean you were just busting my chops before?"

Liz shrugged impishly.

"I shoulda known," Deb groaned.

"All I saw was a shadow, Ben," Liz said. "But I think the man I saw was taller and heavier. Of course I can't be sure. I was in a stupor as well as a state of panic." She was sitting in the chair next to Sadie's desk. Deb was sitting one legged on the corner of the desk where she could glare down at Sadie just to irritate her.

MacCready had sat Liz down where she could see the prisoner when Tom brought him out into the office on the pretense of taking more pictures. He had already taken mug shots the night before.

This way the prisoner would not know that Liz was there to identify him unless he had actually been in her house and had seen her clear enough to recognize. He had walked past her through the area without registering any hint of recognition. He was a slovenly, middle aged man with thick snarled black hair. His face was round and his cheeks hung almost in jowls. His deeply recessed eyes were small, and dark, almost blank. Loose fat jiggled around his neck and belly. He wore a dirty tattered white T-shirt under bib overalls and worn down, run over cowboy boots.

"Now that you mention it," Deb said. "He does look a little puny."

She jumped off the desk and snapped her finger. "Say. Sissy bit the guy that broke in, on his thigh. Did you check this guy?"

Sadie brushed off the corner of the desk where Deb had been sitting.

"No. I don't think so," Ben said.

He motioned to Tom and said, "Tom. Come here, and bring your prisoner with you."

Tom brought the man over. MacCready leaned close to Tom and whispered in his ear. Tom nodded and led the prisoner away. Even in such close proximity, the man had paid no attention to Liz. He did manage a faint sneer at Deb, remembering her from the tractor the night before.

"Who is he?" Liz asked watching Tom lead him away.

"Just some transient. Name's Albert Huntone. Staying at a migrant labor camp just north of town. Says he's been here a few days. On his way south picking up potatoes and whatever other kind of work he can find."

"What was he doing in the neighborhood?" Liz asked.

"Said he was just out walking. Needed to go and popped behind a bush. That's when Tom saw him and took out after him. He claims he was scared, why he ran."

"Pretty far walk from the other side of town," Deb sneered.

"Yeah." The police chief agreed. "He may not be the one who broke into your house, but you can bet he was out looking to steal something from somebody.

"This brings up another angle. Whoever broke into your house and the Drum's may be migrant workers. We may be looking for more than just one person."

Tom Hall returned from putting the prisoner back in his cell at the rear of the building. "No doggie bite on that one, Chief," he said.

"So you caught the wrong man, did you, Sonny," Deb jeered.

"Hey. Wait a minute," Liz said. "What about 'We caught him?'"

Deb ignored the jibe and said to Tom, "Don't you worry, boy. I'll get the job done right for you."

"Thanks, Aunt Deb," Tom said in a tone that showed he was put out, but at the same time well aware that Deb was just being Deb. "That's reassuring."

Chapter Fifteen

"Why did you give the photo album to that weasel?" Deb said as she was driving them back home from the police station.

"I didn't. She took it back."

"You gave it to Sadie?"

"No. The woman we got it from. How'd you know about that?"

"What are you talking about?"

"Well, what are you talking about?" Liz retorted.

"Maybe, you ought to start at the beginning, Liz. You're confusing me."

"I'm confusing you? I'm confused."

"Yeah. That's what I said," Deb agreed. Then she said, "So, how'd MacCready get it?"

"What? The photo album?"

"Well we ain't talkin' about tulips and turnips," Deb sneered.

"Tulips and turnips? What are you talking.....? Never mind. Let's just back up a bit. Are you telling me that Ben MacCready has the photo album?"

"That's right."

"How do you know that?"

"It was lying on his desk, when I peeked in there looking for him, when we first got there this morning. He quickly tossed some papers on top of it when he saw me," Deb explained.

"Are you sure it was the same photo album we had?"

"Sure I'm sure. I'm always sure. Ain't I?"

"Always," Liz agreed sarcastically.

Deb was turning into their driveway now. She pushed the button on the remote to open the garage door.

"Well. How'd he get it?" Liz said more to herself than asking a question of Deb.

"Seems to me, that's what I asked you in the first place."

Deb had just unlocked the side door from the garage to the kitchen and Liz had just managed to ease herself out of the Cherokee, when Marlee Drum entered through the open garage door.

"Good morning, ladies," she greeted. The color in her cheeks was better today and she seemed more upbeat than she had a couple of days before.

"Good morning, Marlee," Liz said as cheerfully as she could. She was hurting bad today and she was still disturbed about the photo album and Ben MacCready. "Come on in. We'll put some coffee on."

"There was quite a commotion over here, last night," Marlee said over the lip of her steaming cup. Then took a tiny sip. Still too hot. "I understand the burglar was caught last night."

"Turns out, it was the wrong man. At least not the one that broke in here," Liz said. She was unwrapping a tootsie pop. Lime again. Not a good day.

"Oh," Marlee said with surprise. "I hadn't heard about that. Did he take anything? I mean. Are you all right?"

"'I'm fine. And no he didn't take anything. Deb and Sissy interrupted him, but he got away."

"But Sissy got a piece of his rump, though," Deb said.

"You mean, she bit him?"

"Got a piece of cloth from his pant leg and spilled blood on the carpet," Deb said proudly.

Marlee's cheeks darkened and her eyes grew dark. "Did you get look at him?" She asked.

"Only shadows," Liz said. "All I could see was he was a big man. That rules out the man they caught last night."

Noticing that Marlee seemed to be upset by all this, Liz said, "I wouldn't worry though, Marlee. With the patrols and all that's been happening around here, I doubt if we'll be having any more problems. Anyone considering a break in must be scared off by now."

"I hope you're right," Marlee said, sounding not quite convinced.

"Something else is bothering you though?" Liz asked. "You mean Lew, don't you?"

"Oh, I don't know. I'm probably making something out of nothing."

"Have you received any more notes?"

"No," she answered. "Maybe, this being Halloween time and all, it was just somebody's idea of a joke."

"Did you bring it up to Lew? I mean, have you confronted him with any of this?" Liz asked.

"No, but I did keep the note. I don't know why I kept it. I just did. I hid it in my jewelry box. Lew never goes in there. I decided not to mention it to him. I didn't think I needed to. Lew's been a good husband. He's taken care of me since I've been sick these past years. I know it has not been easy on him, but he has been loyal and faithful. I shouldn't distrust him now."

"Honey," Deb put in. "He's a man. You can't trust any of them. Believe me I know. After three husbands, I'm an expert on that."

"Well you know what they say about experts?" Liz said and answered it herself. "An expert is someone who knows more and more about less and less until she knows absolutely nothing about anything."

"See I told you I was an expert," Deb said proudly, not getting the gist of it.

"Yeah, you did."

"Lew is a good man," Marlee said. "I never should have doubted him." Then, as an after thought, she said, "He's going to be entertaining at the nursing home for Halloween again this year. That's this Sunday. Will you be going to visit Joe?"

"Oh, I don't know," Liz said wistfully. "I've kind of given up hope." She was silent for a moment. "I suppose I should check in on him though."

"I was kind of hoping to get some time with the tractor this weekend," Deb complained at the prospect of having to drive Liz to the Home.

"You wouldn't have to give that up, Deb," Marlee said. Then to Liz, "Lew said to ask you if you wanted to go with him. He could use the company. I don't feel like going. I think he would like for somebody besides the Home people to see him in his Scooby Doo outfit."

"And just maybe, I could get him talking and see if I think there is anything for you to worry about."

"Well, no. That's not what I meant...."

"I know what you meant," Liz smiled. "And If I feel up to it on Sunday, I'd be glad to let him take me."

"If I were you, I'd watch myself, dearie," Deb put in.

Chapter Sixteen

"Thanks for taking the time to see me, Doctor," Michael Porelli said. He was sitting in front of the desk in Doctor Blakeney's office at the Amity Medical Center. He had introduced himself as Celia Parks' attorney and that he was conducting a preliminary investigation into the incident that caused the death of one Mrs. Jane Pruitt and the suspension of his client from working at the hospital.

"That's quite all right," the physician said. "Celia was a good attendant. Very good at her job. That is until this incident. I still find it hard to believe there was negligence on her part, but mistakes do happen to the best of us." He was a middle age man with a full head of snow white hair that was trimmed neatly and air blown on top. He had a broad face and a square jaw. His complexion was ruddy and free from any facial hair. His sharp blue eyes were prominent, behind contact lenses. His voice was deep and mellow, giving the impression of high intelligence and deep compassion. When he spoke, each word was weighed and delivered with precise deliberation.

"There's no possibility that someone else could have been responsible, I understand there were other attendants present," Michael said, referring to his notes. "A Shirley Robbins and an RN, an N. Taylor."

"Yes. That's Natalie Taylor," Blakeney said.

"I'd like to talk with them if I may," Michael said, writing 'Natalie' in his notes next to the N.

"If Ms. Taylor consents to it, I don't see why not."

"What about Shirley Robbins?"

"I'm afraid she's no longer with us," the doctor said shaking his head.

"Did you dismiss her along with Celia Parks?"

"No," Blakeney said. "She simply left and never came back to work again."

"She left without notice?"

"Precisely."

"Just when was this?

Blakeney reached for his desk calendar and flipped the pages back several days. "Last Monday was the last day she reported for work. She didn't show on Tuesday and we haven't heard from her since."

"Didn't anyone try to contact her?"

"My secretary called her at home and found that the phone was disconnected. Seems she had moved and hadn't notified personnel of her address change and phone number."

"Didn't she have pay coming?"

"No. She wasn't on direct deposit, so she was handed her check here. Payday is twice a month. The fifteenth and the last day of the month. Monday was the fifteenth and she was paid up to date. We don't hold back pay."

"I see," Michael mused. "Apparently, she planned it that way, then. Took the money and ran, so to speak."

"Apparently," the doctor agreed. "She wasn't very good at her job. She seemed to have an attitude and she just didn't seem to care about doing a good job. We're lucky to be rid of her, I guess."

"There's no way she could have been involved in the mix up with the Pruitt woman, then?"

"No." The physician shook his head emphatically. "She had absolutely nothing to do with the patients on that side of the room that day."

"Can you say the same for Ms. Taylor?"

"No, I can't. Ms Taylor was responsible for readying the medications in all of the infusion bags. It was her job to see that the right medication was in the right bag."

"Is it possible, that she could have simply put the wrong medication in the wrong bags?"

"Of course that's possible," Blakeney agreed. "But that's not what happened. The right medications were put in the right bags, but the bags were switched. After Mrs. Pruitt died, the bags were checked and Mrs. Porelli's name was on the bag for Mrs. Pruitt and Mrs. Pruitt's name was on Mrs. Porelli's bag. It was the attendant's job to connect the right bag with the right patient. She must have gotten confused, somehow. Perhaps because their names both began with the letter P. Then again, perhaps Ms. Parks was not functioning with alertness that day. Who knows? She may have been up late the night before. We don't even know if she had any kind of substance abuse problem."

Mike didn't like the insinuation. Celia had not come across to him as someone with a habit. He let it go and said, "Then, there is no doubt in your mind that she simply screwed up?" Michael said.

Blakeney sighed, "I am very much afraid, that is exactly what happened. As you say, she screwed up. Unfortunately, in this business, mistakes can be crucial. And in this case, it was fatal. We all feel terrible for Mrs. Pruitt, but the fact of the matter is that the hospital must not be hampered by this incident. We do far more good than bad, and if we are prevented from doing our jobs, because of an accident, then a lot of people suffer. So you see, the hospital cannot assume all the blame here."

"You mean, you have to have a scape goat?"

"I wouldn't put it that way exactly. After all we must accept the responsibility for our staff and personnel."

"But it does, ease the burden a bit, if the blame can be placed on one person's shoulders."

"The way of the world, Mr. Porelli." He clasped his hands on the top of his desk.

Mike had been gone only seconds. As the doctor's door closed behind him, Blakeney picked up the phone. He punched in a number that he didn't have to look up. He sat impatiently, tapping his toe nervously as he listened to the phone ringing on the other end of the line. After the fourth ring, he heard the receiver on the other end pick up and a voice came on.

"He was just here," Blakeney said, agitated. "He just left."

The voice on the other end said something and Blakeney answered, "No. I didn't tell him any more than I had too. He doesn't seem to know about the girl, though. For some reason, it's been kept quiet, so somebody must know something. That means, she wasn't working alone."

The voice at the other end was calm and reassuring.

"Well, I hope you are able to take care of it. But I'm nervous," Blakeney said.

The voice came back on. Blakeney shook his head as he listened. "Yes, I do trust you. But be careful. That's all I'm saying," he said. There was still doubt in his voice.

"Excuse me," Mike Porelli said as he came up behind the tall blond hair woman in the white uniform of an RN. "Are you Natalie Taylor?"

She turned to face him. She was a striking woman for her mid forties and her face was almost void of lines. Botox, Michael thought. Here is a high maintenance woman.

"Yes,'' she answered. There was a broad smile on her face, but her eyes had a hardness and coldness that belied her sincerity. "What can I do for you?" She held a clipboard in one hand and a pen in the other.

"I'm Michael Porelli," Mike said extended his hand in greeting. "I'm an attorney, gathering information about the incident involving one Mrs. Jane Pruitt."

The woman merely glanced at his hand dismissively and failed to return the gesture. "Pruitt family attorney? So there is going to be a law suit after all? I thought there wasn't going to be any."

"No Ms. Taylor," Michael said quickly before the woman got carried any further away with the wrong conclusions. "I'm not representing the Pruitts. I'm just gathering information, in case there are any legal ramifications."

"Then you represent the hospital. Why didn't you say so in the first place?"

"I'm afraid you've still got it wrong. I don't represent the hospital either."

Her heavily mascarade eyes flashed with a bit of temper. "Then who sent you? Just who are you working for?"

"I'm afraid I can't tell you that just yet, but I would like to ask you a few questions."

"Well, you certainly are one most afraid man. I'll give you that. Well, I'm also afraid. I'm afraid

I can't answer any questions from just anybody. Especially, when I don't know who you represent." She started to turn and walk away.

"Who told you there wasn't going to be a law suit?" Michael asked sharply as she turned.

She halted and turned back toward him. "I never said anyone told me that," she snapped.

"Did someone here in the hospital tell you?" Michael asked sharply.

"No." She leveled her gaze at him. "It's been very quiet around here. I just assumed that it was all blowing over." She seemed very nervous and defensive.

"Is that what usually happens when someone dies by mistake? It just blows over?"

"I don't think I like you Mr. Por......, or what ever you said your name was. And don't come around here again with your silly questions. I don't have to answer them," she said. Then she turned once again and stomped off down the hallway.

"We'll see about that Ms. Taylor," Michael thought to himself. "We'll see."

Chapter Seventeen

It was already starting to get dark at four thirty in the afternoon. It would be even darker at this time in another week or so. Liz always hated the change from daylight savings time to standard time. It always made the day seem so short and night so long. And she dreaded having to change the clocks. She knew she would have to do this soon.

She had woken up early that morning, remembering that it was Sunday and that she was going to go to the nursing home to visit Joe. She was hurting bad today and the change in temperature had not helped one bit. There had been a frost the night before and the grass was still dusted with white when she had first looked out in the morning. Just the sight of it had made her feel colder, even though she had a warm house.

Marlee Drum had just called to tell her that Lew would be ready to leave for the home at six.

Deb had been outside all afternoon with her tractor and when she finally put it away and came in, it was a few minutes before six. Liz already had her long, dark blue winter coat on. This was the first she had worn it this year. As she peered out the front room window, she was wishing to herself that she had declined Lew Drum's offer to drive her to the home. It always depressed her to see Joe the way he was. Especially when she wasn't feeling well. And, she hadn't been feeling well for several days now. Today, her eyesight was a bit blurred in her right eye. She felt light headed and a bit dizzy.

The garage light went on next door and Lew Drum emerged carrying a suitcase. She saw Marlee open the front door and stepped halfway out on the stoop.

She waved to Lew, but Lew was busy settling himself in the car and didn't seem to notice or perhaps, he just didn't bother to wave.

Liz started for the front door. "There's Lew, now," Liz said. "I'd better get out there."

"Call me if you need me," Deb said, taking off her heavy jacket and pile hat, hanging them up on a hook in the kitchen.

By the time Liz got outside, Lew Drum had already started his car, backed out of his driveway and had driven into Liz's, so she wouldn't have to walk any farther than necessary.

"Lew always was considerate and thoughtful," Liz mused.

"Can you help me a bit with this, Liz?" Lew Drum asked as he came out of the men's room. Liz had been waiting in the hallway for him to change into his costume. He was wearing a baggy brown and black body suit with doggie feet. He held the head of a giant Scooby Doo in his hands. "I always have trouble getting the zipper in the back all the way up. I just can't seem to reach it." He turned his back to her. The zipper was about two thirds up, leaving it V'd open exposing the back of his white shirt.

She zipped it all the way to the nape of his neck and fastened the zipper mechanism tight so it wouldn't slide down. "There you are," Liz said, smoothing out the fabric of the costume across his broad shoulders.

"Thanks," he said as he lifted the Scooby head and placed it over his own settling the bottom flaps on his shoulders. "How do I look?" He asked, turning around to face her.

"Like a giant Scooby. If I didn't know it was you in that getup, I'd never suspect it was you."

"Good or should I say Rood? Row's rabout rum rambergers." He did a good job of sounding like Scooby.

Liz laughed.

Lew said, "I guess I should be getting down to the day room about now. My audience awaits." He turned and waddled down the hallway.

"He's such a good sport to do this for these old people every year. A man of his position in the community, willing to go to such lengths to entertain," Liz thought to herself as she watched him go. She had always liked Lew Drum. She had been shocked when Marlee told her of her suspicions and there was no way she could ever bring herself to believe Lew was that kind of man.

On the way over to the home, her conversation with Lew was light and congenial as always. She didn't get any vibes or sense that anything was wrong between him and Marlee. Wherever that strange note had come from, she was almost sure that it did not mean that Lew was cheating on his wife. For some reason, someone was merely trying to cause trouble for the couple. Perhaps an irate customer at the bank may have wanted to get even with Lew for what ever wrong he perceived Lew as committing.

Lew could walk much faster, even in his doggie feet than Liz could travel the length of the hallway with her cane. Scooby was already in action with his antics in the day room by the time Liz got there and hung her coat up on the coat racks near the front door of the home.

The day room was a large open bay area with several stuffed chairs and sofas scattered about. There was a large screen HD television set against the far wall. It was on with CNN news, but the volume had been turned down for Scooby's performance.

The room was filled with residents. Some sat in the chairs and sofas with their walkers and canes parked near them. Others lined the wall of the hallway in wheel chairs. While some of the patients were cognizant enough to laugh and respond to Scooby, many remained unable to register any response at all. Liz hated to see people like this, so she hurried passed the day room down the hallway into the next wing where Joe's room was located.

It had been at least three months since Liz had visited her husband. She found his room; the third one from the end of the hall on the left. The door was wide open as usual and she could hear the low droning sound of the TV that was always on whether Joe knew it was or not. She stood in the open doorway for a moment, gazing at the remnants of the man that had been her husband for so many years. He looked the same as the last time. Frail and pale. Propped up in a high backed stuffed chair and strapped in so he wouldn't slide out. His hair was mostly gone, now. Just a few wispy strands of gray, was all that was left of the curly jet black hair he had sported as a young man. His arms were draped over the arms of the chair and his fingers twitched uncontrollably. His head drooped; his chin almost lying against his chest. His eyes stared downward at his feet and a trace of spittle leaked from the right corner of his mouth.

Even though he looked as he always did and the way she expected, Liz still felt the same feeling of shock as she stood in the doorway looking at him. A lump rose in her throat and her eyes watered. The dizziness she had been experiencing seemed to increase and waved over her. She felt herself falling sideways and leaned against the door jam, moving her cane a little bit in front of her to steady herself. Her breath caught for a moment and she closed her eyes. She rested against the side of the door for a moment. Then as her breath returned, she gradually opened her eyes. She gripped her cane a little tighter and grasped the side of the door jam with her other hand. The dizziness was subsiding to the level she had been suffering earlier.

"Joe," she finally said. "It's me, Liz." Her voice was but a croak.

He didn't move. Just continued to stare in the same position. There was no sign of recognition or response on his part.

Slowly she moved into the room. There was a straight back chair next to his bed that she usually used whenever she came to visit. She slid it over beside and almost in front of Joe. There was no indication that he was aware of the movement.

She lowered herself gingerly into the chair, keeping the quad cane in front of her. She leaned over and looked up into her husband's face. She fought back the urge to cry.

She took a Kleenex from her pocket and dabbed at the spittle on his lips. His cheeks quivered a bit. Then she folded the tissue to a dryer side and wiped the poor man's brow. His eyes rolled upward as if looking up into her face.

Her heart almost leaped into her throat as she thought she detected a faint light in the eyes. She swallowed it back, fighting the urge to even hope that he was beginning to show a hint of recognition. She knew it was not possible. Not now. Not ever. Her lips quivered and the ends turned sharply downward. She could no longer hold back the tears. She wept bitterly and cradled his head in her arms.

Over an hour had passed by the time Liz had left Joe's room and returned to the day room. At first she did not see Scooby, but after a moment he reappeared, coming down the hallway back into the day room. He was carrying a basket of goodies that he had been distributing throughout the home and was now dispensing the leftovers to the remaining residents in the day room.

Liz was tired. So very tired. She practically fell into one of the vacant stuffed chairs and sank into the softness of the cushions. She buried her aching head into the back of the chair. She could go to sleep easily, she thought.

Scooby tossed some fun size candy bars in her lap as he went by. A Snickers bar, a Three Musketeers and two Milky Way dark chocolate. She smiled back as Lew Drum as Scooby danced on to the other residents and even the staff until the candy was all gone.

"I'll be right back, Lew said from behind his Scooby mask as he came back close to her. "As soon as I change we can get going." He hurried on down the hallway into the men's room to change.

"That's strange," Lew said as he drove into his driveway. "Marlee's got all the lights off." The house was totally dark, but the front window drapes were still open.

"Maybe she's gone to bed," Liz said.

"It's still early yet. Besides, she said she would wait up for me. I hope nothing's wrong," he said almost to himself, concern rising in his tone. "But I thought she was feeling pretty good today."

"Maybe she fell asleep in a chair watching television before it got dark," Liz said trying to reassure him.

"No." He shook his head. "It was getting dark before we left. Remember? The lights were already on."

"Well there's no point sitting here wondering," Liz said. "Let's get in there and find out."

"You're right," Lew agreed pressing the button of the garage door opener and then opening the car door and sliding out. He moved slowly as if afraid of finding out that his fears were founded.

"You want me to come too?" Liz asked, already climbing out of the door. The garage door motor was already buzzing as the big panel rolled upward. The sound stopped and the door locked into place in its track near the ceiling. The garage light went on automatically.

Lew Drum moved slowly across the garage floor toward the stairs of three steps that led to the side door into the kitchen. Liz shuffled quickly behind him and caught up with him as he opened the door. He reached inside the door to the left, felt for the light switch and flicked it on. The overhead kitchen light filtered into the dining room, living room and hall beyond.

"Marlee?" Lew called. There was a tremor in his voice.

Liz followed him into the kitchen. There was no answer from Marlee. The house was quiet except for the blaring rush of the furnace motor that seemed to be working overtime, keeping up the temperature. Blasts of cold air rushed in from somewhere in the dining room.

As they entered the dining room, they could see the sliding glass door on the outside wall had been broken and stood wide open. Shards of glass were strewn all over the carpet and the drapes whipped wildly about from the incoming breeze. Lew quickly flicked on the dining room light switch; once again crying out "Marlee!" Urgency had risen in his voice.

"Oh, my God!" Liz exclaimed as she glanced into the living room.

Lew Drum turned, his face ashen white and he was shaking. He saw it too. The room was a mess. Lamps lay broken on the floor, the carpet torn and furniture turned over. And in the middle of the living room floor, lying in a crumpled heap was the slim form of Marlee Drum. She was lying very still, in a curled up fetal position, on the floor. Her eyes were fixed wide open with a sightless glare and her hair was matted with a dark stain. There were several deep gashes in the back of her head. A large dark pool of blood had spread out in a large circle beneath her, soaking deeply into the carpet and was already starting to dry. She had died quickly.

Chapter Eighteen

Marlee Drum was buried on Wednesday. Strange how life tends to stand still when death arrives. The sunlight, the air, the general feel of everything seems to be a bit abstract; heightened awareness of the world about, yet a strange detachment from this world and a wanting loneliness of something totally indefinable. Life goes on. It drags at a snail's pace at first, then whizzes by with incredible speed until suddenly the visitation of death is long gone and the void left behind becomes only fleeting memories of a time that hardly existed.

Marlee's son and his family from Tucson had flown in for the funeral as had her two daughters and their families, from Richmond and Atlanta. Marlee's marriage to Lew was her second and she and Lew had never had any children together, in that they had married each other rather late in life after each one had suffered marital collapses with former spouses. Lew had no other children with his first wife. Marlee's ex husband had no interest in attending the funeral and her son and daughters flew home quickly after the funeral.

Lew had decided that it would be unbearable to stay in the house alone, so he took a room at a hotel downtown for the time being.

The funeral had been a plain affair, although the attendance was high given Lew's position in the community. Marlee had always stayed home and did not have a lot of acquaintances outside of the neighborhood.

Liz asked Lew if he would like her to ask her nephew Father Frank to officiate at the funeral services and he seemed thankful for the offer.

For late October when the skies were usually drab and cold, they had expected the bleak prospect of rain that always cast such a dreadful pall over a cemetery. But contrary to the expectations, the day was sunny and bright giving an orangey sheen to the remaining leaves on the trees. The air carried a crisp chill though, and the grim gathering of mourners crowded beneath the tent near the grave sight.

Lew Drum stood off by himself while Marlee's children gathered in their own circle offering no comfort to the lonely man.

Liz and Deb were at the rear of the crowd, outside the tent. James and his wife Vera stood with them along with Michael Porelli.

Father Frank had rendered a touching farewell and the mourners drifted away family by family. Lew Drum remained for a while, staring at the casket. Martin and Roger Callan were the last to walk up to Lew, shake his hand and offer their condolences. After a brief conversation, Martin patted Lew gently on the back in a reassuring gesture. Then he and his son returned to their car and drove away. Lew watched them go, then hunched up his shoulders as if adjusting his coat and strode off to his own car. He drove away by himself. A lonely man.

The portly young priest stayed behind. Liz and Deb had invited Frank, Mike, Jim and Vera back to her house for coffee and doughnuts. Mike had indicated earlier that he needed to talk with Liz about the situation at the hospital. He had refrained for a few days, knowing Liz was caught up in the tragic death of Marlee Drum. He had expected Liz would be doing poorly these days as the stress would usually induce the return of her MS. Ironically, the monster had not returned and Liz exuded a strength that he would not have expected.

Finding Marlee's body was a shock. She had never experienced anything like this before. Instead of weakening under the stress, she had thought only of Lew Drum and had done her best to console him and help him notify the authorities when he didn't seem to be up to it.

It had been midnight that Sunday, before the coroner took away the body and Liz was able to go to her own home and get to bed. She was exhausted from the ordeal, not to mention that she was way past her usual sleeping time.

She paid for it the next day. She slept all day, awaking catatonic for several hours, but gradually she bounced back, even though she had missed her medications for a day and a half.

"So how is the old man doing, these days?" Frank Porelli asked of Michael. They were sitting in the kitchen. Deb had brought in two additional folding chairs and had crowded everyone around the table. Coffee cups were steaming and an open box of doughnuts sat in the center of the table.

"Still owes his soul to the devil," Mike quipped flippantly. "Too bad you can't do something about that."

"Saving souls may be my business, Mikey." Father Frank had a jovial round face and dark rimmed glasses that sat on puffy cheeks. "But, I'm a miserable failure when it comes to my own family."

"Don't I count for something?" Mike said. "Or don't you figure I've been saved?"

"You didn't need saving, Mikey. Except from the old man. You always knew where the right road was."

"Thanks for coming, Frank," Liz interrupted. "I'm sure it meant a lot to Lew Drum."

"I hope so," the priest said. "I was glad to do it. Gave me a chance to see all of you again. Since I went off to Buffalo, I don't seem to get down this way much. I know it's not that far, but my parish keeps me very busy." Then he added, "Besides, anytime my favorite aunt asks me for a favor, I can't refuse."

"Seems to me, I'm your only aunt," Liz said.
"That's why you're his favorite, Liz," Deb piped up. "You wouldn't be if you had any competition."

"All kidding aside, Aunt Liz," Frank's dark eyes softened and a little of the gleam dissipated. "How are you? You've had a really tough time lately with the trouble at the hospital and the break-in last week. And now this. I really didn't expect you to be holding up this well."

"To tell the truth," Liz said. "I'm not. Haven't had even one lollipop today. I'm starting to have withdrawal pangs." She turned in her chair and reached for the candy dish. She offered it to everyone else, but still busy with coffee and doughnuts, they declined.

She put the dish away and then unwrapped the pop. Cherry. Maybe things were looking up.

"Have you talked with Celia, lately?" Michael asked after the others had left. They were sitting in the living room now. Michael was sitting in Liz's usual chair and Liz was in Sissy's and holding the little pug on her lap. She stroked Sissy gently and the little dog squinted her eyes, relishing the touch. Deb was out back with her tractor.

"Yes. I called her yesterday afternoon to tell her what had happened around here and to ask her if she had had any more problems."

"You mean about being followed and watched?"

"Yes. She said she hadn't seen anything strange since that one night."

"She didn't tell you that I went to see her day before yesterday?"

"No. No she didn't," Liz seemed concerned.

"No need to be concerned," Michael said. "In light of what's been happening to you lately, she just probably forgot to mention it. I only asked, because I didn't know if you already knew what I went to see her about."

"Well what was it?"

"Do you remember the other attendant that day at the hospital? The one that didn't work on you that day, but had before."

"Yes. Of course. She had put the needle in my arm in a most uncomfortable manner. Celia fixed it for me."

"Well I went to the hospital and talked with..." His words were cut off by the ringing of the door-bell. "Were you expecting someone?" Mike asked.

"No, I wasn't." She started to get up.

"Stay put," he said. "I'll get it."

When he swung the door open, he saw Chief of Police Ben MacCready standing on the stoop. "It's MacCready," he said to Liz. He opened the storm door.

"I'd like to speak with Liz, if she's up to it," MacCready said in an official tone.

"Let him in, Mike. I'm okay." She would say she was, even if she had a knife in her heart.

"All right. Come on in. As long as you don't stay too long." Mike pushed the storm door open wider. Mike stepped back as the big man came inside.

MacCready removed his hat as he saw Liz sitting in the chair. "Hello, Liz," he said less officially, almost sincerely apologetic.

"Hello, Mac," Liz said. "I was wondering when you were going to get around to this. I suppose you've got questions for me."

"Yes," he answered. "I didn't want to put you through it earlier. I was hoping that by now you'd be up to it."

"I'm fine, Mac," Liz said. "Come in and sit down."

He glanced at Michael apprehensively and moved past him toward the chair that Liz had indicated.

"You know my nephew, Michael, of course?" It was more of a statement than a question.

"Yes, I'm quite familiar with him and his Dad," the police chief said with disdain. Then to Michael, "Your father and I have had many occasions to meet."

"I'm sure you have," Michael mused.

"One day I'll nail his ornery hide," MacCready said, menacingly, indicating that it might be Michael's hide as well.

Liz started to protest, but Mike held up a palm. "It's okay, Liz. It's his job. No offense taken."

Mike nodded to the lawman, dismissively. "Well I'd better be going, Liz. I'll talk to you later." He picked up his overcoat from the arm of the chair, shrugged into it and left.

"I'm sorry, Liz," Ben apologized. "It's just that Vinnie Porelli has been a thorn in my side for such along time."

"I've told you many times before, Ben," Liz said, still a bit put out with his attitude toward Mike. "Michael and I are not a part of Vinnie's shady enterprises."

"Oh, I believe you Liz," he retorted. "I must admit there was a time when I didn't, but no more."

"What changed your mind?"

"I guess I've just gotten too old to want to jump at shadows like I used too." He seemed genuinely apologetic.

Liz said, "So why don't you sit down and tell me what's on your mind?"

The big man shrugged off his leather police jacket and dropped into the stuffed chair that Michael had just vacated.

Sissy Boom Boom's eyes opened and saw the man. Her skin tightened and a low growl started in her throat. Then with a sudden jolt, she leaped from Liz's lap, hitting the carpet on a run and scampered out into the kitchen, no longer in view.

"Looks like your dog doesn't like me much," MacCready said.

"She's usually a good judge of character," Liz said absently, not realizing how it sounded at first, then saying, "Oh, I didn't mean to ...."

"I know, Liz. Forget it." He took a notepad out of his pocket and pen from his shirt pocket. "Now could you tell me about the other night? What you saw, heard, anything that might help me understand just what happened."

Liz explained how she had talked to Marlee on the phone about four thirty on Sunday. How Lew had driven her to the nursing home and brought her back. How they had found Marlee's body and the house torn apart as if it had been burglarized.

MacCready listened intently, taking notes occasionally. When Liz had apparently finished, the policeman asked, "Are you sure she was still alive when you left with Lew Drum?"

"You're not suggesting that Lew had anything to do with her death?" Liz flashed angrily.

"I..I'm just asking questions," MacCready held up both hands in defense. "I'm not suggesting anything. I just have to cover all possibilities. That's all."

Liz settled down and said, "I suppose you have to." Then she said, "Marlee opened the front door and waved to Lew when he was leaving. Of course she was still alive."

"You saw her plainly? You're sure it was her?"

"Positive," Liz said. "No doubt about it."

MacCready wrote something on his pad, then said, "Now Liz, don't get upset about this, but I have to ask it. Do you know if Lew and Marlee were having any problems?"

"Seems to me, that's something you should be asking Lew Drum, himself." Liz said emphatically and not answering the question.

"I have," MacCready said. "And he said there was nothing really. He did admit that it had been difficult dealing with Marlee's illnesses. I just wondered if you had anything to add to that or if you had noticed anything. I know you and Marlee were good friends. Did she ever confide in you about anything?"

Liz thought about the note and Marlee's concerns. Did she dare tell MacCready about it? Instead of a direct answer, she responded. "So, you are considering Lew a suspect?" She almost sneered.

"Unfortunately, in any case like this, the spouse is always the first to be suspected. It's just procedure to rule it out. You seem to have done a good job of convincing me that Lew couldn't have had anything to do with it. He certainly couldn't have been in two places at the same time."

"What about the break-ins and the burglary? You don't think that's what it was all about?"

MacCready sighed. "It looks like that is exactly what happened. The house had been ransacked and several valuable items were missing. Marlee's jewelry box was completely empty."

Liz waited for the policeman to say something about the note that Marlee had hidden it the jewelry box. When he didn't she wondered if he had found it and was just not mentioning it. As he continued talking, she decided, perhaps the note wasn't there. The burglar may have just dumped everything into a bag or something, without noticing it. At any rate, she had decided not to mention anything about it.

"I had Tom go out to pick up Albert Huntone." Liz heard MacCready say above her thoughts. She put her attention on the police chief and listened. "But it seems, he's already skipped town."

"You think it could have been him?" Liz asked.

"Quite possible. We're not ruling it out. It could also be almost anyone else too. Right now we don't have much to go on. But I promise you this. I won't let this case be closed until I find the person or persons responsible for Marlee Drum's death."

Chapter Nineteen

"What are you doing down there?" Deb Raymond said as she came in to the kitchen from outdoors. Sissy Boom Boom was on the floor, cringing in the corner. Her nose was wedged between the cabinets on each side and her paws were folded over her eyes.

A blast of cold air came from the front room and Deb looked up to see Ben MacCready leaving. He pulled the door shut behind him and the cold air went with it.

"Did you ask him about the photo album?' Deb said, pulling off the scarf from around her neck. Her cheeks were still red from the brisk outdoor air.

Liz was still sitting in Sissy's chair, watching through the front room picture window as Ben MacCready backed the black and white police car out of the driveway and drove off down the street. Deb glanced out the window, watching the policeman go.

"Wh..What?" Liz said absently, jerking her head up suddenly. She had been thinking intently.

"Did you ask him about the album?" Deb repeated.

"No. I didn't," Liz said. "I totally forgot about it." Then she said, "I don't know how I would have brought it up to him anyhow. Kinda awkward, don't you think?"

"Not to a slime ball like him," Deb said. "I'd've just asked him straight out."

"Yeah, I know you would've. But I guess I just don't have your tact."

Deb ignored the insinuation. "I sure would like to know who that broad was in that picture with him."

"I'd forgotten about that to," Liz mumbled almost to herself, then, she said to Deb. "You know how I said she looked like someone at the hospital?" She didn't wait for an answer. "Michael was asking me about her just before Mac-Cready came."

"Mike knows about the girl in the picture?"

"No. I mean about the girl at the hospital. He never did tell me what that was all about. I wonder if..." She reached for the handheld phone and punched in Michael's office number. She glanced at her watch as she listened to the ring at the other end of the line. Mike had probably not had enough time to get back to his office by now, but it was worth a try.

Michael's secretary came on the line. Liz said, "Hello. Peggy? Is Mike back yet? He left here a little while ago."

"Not yet, Liz. I don't expect him back for a while. He was going someplace else after your place. I can have him call you when he gets back."

"Thanks. In the meantime I'll try his cell." Liz hung up and punched in the cell number. His phone was off and went straight to voicemail. "Mike. This is Liz. Call me as soon as you can." She hung up again and put the hand held back in its cradle.

"What's going on?" Deb asked.

"I don't know. But I've got a feeling." She picked up the phone again and said. "Deb, be a peach and hand me the notepad that's next to the phone in the kitchen."

"You mean this one?" Deb said bringing a narrow yellow pad. The name Celia Parks was written on it along with a phone number. Liz took it and punched the number.

"Hello. Celia?" Liz said when a voice answered. "This is Liz. How are things?"

"Quiet and boring," she answered. "I've been staying in most of the time. I haven't seen that man who was watching me since that first time. Maybe I was just jumping at shadows, after all. How are you doing? I hear things have been happening. Michael was here to see me and he told me about them."

"That's what I wanted to talk to you about, Celia. Michael said he talked to you and he asked me about the other attendant at the hospital, but he didn't get a chance to tell me what it was all about. I thought maybe you could fill me in."

"I don't know much about it. All Michael said was that Shirley Robbins, that's the other attendant, seems to be missing. No one seems to know where she is. I think Michael thinks there's something suspicious about it. But he didn't tell me what it was that he was thinking."

"Thanks, Celia," Liz said hurriedly wanting to get off the phone. "Talk to you later. Take care now."

"So what's the scoop?" Deb asked.

Liz put the phone down and picked up another lollipop. "You know what I think?" She said as she unwrapped the pop.

"That's what I've been asking you," Deb said impatiently.

"I think the girl in that picture is the same one from the hospital." She put the pop in her mouth. Cherry. Yeah things were starting to look up.

"So what?" Deb said.

"So she's missing, that's what. And I think our dear chief of police knows it."

"You think MacCready had something to do with what happened at the hospital?"

"I don't know what to think," Liz said. "It hardly seems possible. Not even likely."

"Maybe what happened at the hospital wasn't an accident at all," Deb said. "Maybe you were supposed to die after all. The bags got mixed up and the wrong broad died."

"That's silly, Deb. Who'd want to kill me?"

"Ben MacCready, of course."

"That's even sillier," Liz scoffed. "Why would he want to kill me?"

"Who knows about that piece of slime," Deb answered. "He's just a mean son of a bitch. He don't need no reason. Besides, he never did like Joe. Hey. Maybe he's the one who hurt Joe too."

"Now you're letting your imagination run wild. That wouldn't make sense, either."

"He got Joe's job didn't he?"

"Well, yes. But he wouldn't kill to get it. People don't do that over just a job."

"Don't kid yourself. People have killed over a lot less. Just look at the evidence."

"You're playing cop again, I suppose," Liz said. "What evidence?'

"You said yourself, the man that broke in was about MacCready's size."

"Doesn't make sense. He's the chief of police. He makes a good salary. Why would he turn to burglary?"

"Don't you see? It wasn't burglary at all. He was trying to kill you. It didn't work the first time at the hospital, so he tried it again. Remember, Sissy bit the man? Well when I saw Mac-Cready the next morning he was favoring his right hip. Just about the same place where Sissy got a piece of him. And just now Sissy was hiding from him in the kitchen."

The pooch came back in the front room, her tail wagging. She had heard them talking about her.

"That could have been a coincidence. He could have hurt himself some other way. Yet Sissy doesn't seem to like him much."

"That makes two of us," Deb said. "He did say he hurt himself at an accident site the day before. You know when that girl was killed."

"That's right. There was an accident that day," Liz mused. "We never did hear who she was, and Ben was evasive when I asked him about that. I wonder...."

"Wonder what?"

"Oh, nothing. Besides, all this talk is ridiculous anyhow. Have you been reading my Nancy Drew books?"

"Nah, I wouldn't read that crap." Deb answered.

Deb was silent for a bit, thinking about the possibility. After a few moments she said, "What about the other break ins? You think he did that too? Surely, you don't think he killed Marlee."

"Nah. He just took advantage of it. After the first break in, he just figured everyone would naturally assume it was the same burglar. He missed at the Hospital and took advantage of the break in at Drum's to try again."

"But he wasn't even at the hospital."

"Ah, but maybe he has a girlfriend there. Maybe he had her set up the infusion bag with something that would kill you."

"Nonsense. The hospital determined that it was a reaction to my medication that killed the Pruitt woman. I'd had it several times and had no such reaction."

"What if there was something else in the bag that time? Like a poison or something."

"The hospital would have discovered it."

"Maybe they did. You never heard of a cover up?"

"You're just imagining things, now, Deb."

"Yeah? Well then, you tell me what happened to Shirley Robbins?"

Amalgamated Concrete Delivery did not look like a thriving business from the outside. The entire site including building and parking lot probably covered less than an acre, fenced in by a high chain link fence. Three strands of barb wire were stretched above it to keep trespassers out. It was in a rundown neighborhood bordering the southern fringes of Buffalo, just below the thruway. The building was a squat one story building, almost square in shape. Its cinder block walls were dingy from grime and age.

Four concrete delivery trucks were in the back lot. Two were obviously parked and out of service for the time being and the other two were loaded with concrete. Their engines were running and the giant drums were turning, keeping the concrete moist and porous.

Michael Porelli parked his car next to a red Porche near the entrance to the building and went inside. The inside was rundown and furniture was sparse.

"You must have an appointment to see Mr. Pruitt," the snip of a young girl at the reception desk said, not too politely. She was thin and short. Her dark hair hung straight, neck length.

"Just tell him Vinnie Porelli's attorney is here," Michael said. "He'll see me."

The girl stared at him. "No he won't."

"Just buzz him," Mike said sounding secretive. "He'll see me."

The girl grimaced, then picked up the phone receiver and pushed a button on the console. She turned away from Michael and spoke into the phone. Her head nodded a few times during the short conversation. She hung up and swung around to face Michael. She glared angrily. She didn't like to be wrong. "He'll be right out," she said.

"What the hell!" Arnold Pruitt shouted as he came storming around the corner of his battle scarred old wooden desk. He was a short middle aged man with a lot of flab hanging over his belt. A black goatee on his round chin matched his greasy hair and the bushy drooping mustache that spread out beneath his fat cheeks. His dark eyebrows were just as bushy and his arms that protruded from the rolled up sleeves of his denim shirt were covered with dark hair. "You said Vinnie sent you. And here you are asking me all theses questions."

Mike cowered back a little in the wooden straight chair he was sitting in, before Pruitt's desk. He didn't retaliate at first. He just let the man rant.

"It's none of your business, if I decide not to sue the hospital. You have your nerve coming in here and making insinuations. If you hadn't said Vinnie sent you, I never would have let you in."

"I never actually said Vinnie sent me," Mike said. "I only said that I was Vinnie's attorney. I didn't know for sure that you even knew Vinnie. I just thought that considering the business you're in, it was quite possible that you two were..."

"Connected," Pruitt said. "You think I'm mob, just because I'm in construction?"

"Well, I could ask my father."

"Go ahead. He'll tell you we've had business before, but that's all. I do a lot of work for all kinds of businesses."

"You've had contracts with Amity Hospital?"

"Of course. They need concrete when they build."

"Is that why you're not suing the hospital."

"I never said I wasn't. Who told you that?" Arnold Pruit came back.

Mike didn't answer the question directly. He said, "Seems to me, most people wouldn't take their wife's death so lightly that they wouldn't want to seek retribution from those responsible for it."

"What are you saying? Can't you see how broken up I am about this. My wife meant everything to me."

"Sure," Michael said. "I can see that. I'll bet her money meant even more."

"What money? We've been near broke for over a year now. Business has been bad."

"Then that four hundred thousand dollar policy you took out on her last June, should help out a lot."

"Are you saying I had something to do with my wife's death?"

Mike didn't answer and Pruitt continued. "How could I? I wasn't even there. Besides it was an accident. The hospital screwed up."

"Maybe you knew someone there who could help with the accident. Maybe you know a Shirley Robbins."

Pruit stepped closer, his massive fists balled, fire in his eyes. "That's enough punk. Get out of here! Now! And tell Vinnie I'll be seeing him real soon."

Chapter Twenty

"Are you sure you're going to be all right, Liz?" Deb said from behind the wheel of the Cherokee as Liz pushed the passenger side door wide open and placed her cane on the pavement below. She gripped hard on the metal hand rail that had been installed on the inside of the door. Her grip was weak and her head felt light and she was dizzy. The street lights and the lights from Amity Hospital were like dancing orbs reflecting in her brain against the black backdrop of night.

"I...I'll be fine, Deb. Don't worry about me."

"Wait a minute, Liz. Let me get over there and help you down." She was already getting out of the SUV.

The Cherokee was sitting in the circle at the front entrance to the hospital. The night air was biting cold at this time of night.

It had been four o'clock in the afternoon when Liz had finally settled down for her long overdue nap. She had finally caught up with her medication that she had missed the last couple of days and had gone to bed. Her sleep had been fitful and she had terrible dreams that she would not remember upon wakening at six o'clock when Deb had awoken her to take an important phone call.

"Hello, Francis," Liz had mumbled through the haze of half wakefulness. It was Father Frank.

"Liz," he said as she came on the line. "Michael has had a bad accident and is at Amity Hospital, here in Buffalo.

Liz had jerked instantly awake at that. Her concern over shadowed the throbbing pain in her head and neck and she ignored the blurred vision in her right eye.

"Wh...what happened?"

"We're not sure yet, but his car is a total wreck. Mike is in surgery right now. He hasn't been conscious enough to tell us anything. He did mumble your name and we did find your message on his cell phone. I thought you should know what happened."

"You were right about that," Liz said. "Will he be all right?"

"We don't know. He's got broken bones, but I don't know if there is anything life threatening yet."

"I'll be right there," Liz said. "Thanks for letting me know."

"I don't know if it's necessary that you come here. You need to take care of yourself. There's nothing you can do, here. I just thought you should know."

"Just the same, I'll be right there. I need to."

As soon as she had gotten off the phone to Father Frank, she called Celia Parks and told her what had happened. She asked if she could stay with her if she didn't stay at the hospital all night. She told her that Deb would drive her to the hospital, but couldn't stay, as she would need to get back home and get some sleep, before going to work, in the morning. She had already lost too much time at work lately. Celia agreed and Liz had told her that she would give her a call from the hospital if she needed her.

Liz had tried to rest during the trip to Buffalo and she had drifted in and out of sleep; the street lights and lights of passing cars continually floating in and out of her consciousness.

Now as Deb helped her down from the Cherokee, Liz could hardly feel her numbing feet hit the black top, and she wondered if she could actually fend for herself now, but she refused to admit it to Deb. "Don't worry about me," she said as Deb helped her step up onto the concrete walk. The automatic door in front of her slid open at the motion. She shook Deb off. "I'll call you," she said, looking straight ahead and not bothering to look back at Deb as she shuffled through the door and stepped into the inner revolving door. The sliding door closed behind her.

Liz grabbed a wheel chair from the lobby so she could have a chair to lean on and a seat to sit on, in case she got weak.

Deb watched for a few moments as Liz crossed the lobby floor and approached the reception desk. She finally left when she saw Liz speaking to the receptionist.

Liz was directed to the fourth floor via the blue elevators, which was the first bank of elevators, not far down the main corridor to the right.

When Liz stepped off the elevator on the fourth floor, she turned into the corridor to the left. From here she could see the nurse's station off to the right at the far end of the hall. Standing in the open area in front of the nurse's desk were two men that she recognized right away; Vinnie Porelli, which was hardly surprising that he would be there for his son, but it was surprising that the other man was Mandalyn's Chief of Police, Ben MacCready.

MacCready was out of uniform, wearing a black leather jacket and black pants. His arms were moving about emphasizing a very animated and perhaps heated conversation with the elder Porelli.

The conversation seemed to end abruptly when they saw Liz approaching. Liz pushed the wheel chair off to the side of the corridor. Her cane was in her right hand and she leaned heavily on it. She walked close to the left wall so her left hand could occasionally touch it and give her some added stability. The dizziness was still with her.

Vinnie abruptly walked away from Mac-Cready, taking long deliberate strides toward Liz. "Who the hell asked you to come here?" He fumed. Without waiting, nor expecting an answer he continued, "You've already done enough.

If he hadn't been out nosing into things for you, this would never have happened."

'It's good to see you again too," Liz said sarcastically; halting and bracing herself against the wall with her left palm. "How is he?" She totally ignored Vinnie's wrath.

"He just came out of recovery and isn't conscious, yet. We won't know for awhile." His flabby face was gray with concern and Liz could see something what she rarely saw in the big tough guy; fear. Then he caught himself and screwed his face back into a stoic mask.

"I suppose that lily livered son of mine called you, didn't he?" Vinnie always hated it that Francis had turned away from him and had joined the priesthood, but, when he would speak in public about his son, he always exuded a tone of pride. And that was not fake, for deep inside, he felt he had a link to the great almighty, despite his ways on this earth. "Well," he continued. "You might as well, go back home. I don't want you hanging around here with me."

"Don't worry, Vinnie. I won't bother you. I just want to be here for Michael."

"That could be some time yet. You go on home. I'll call you when I know something."

"You mean, I can't see him?"

"Not now, I'll let you know." He turned and started to move away.

"I'm staying in town tonight." She released her cane and lifted her purse. She reached inside and pulled out a small note pad and pen as she stumbled forward. She quickly wrote down Celia's number and handed the slip of paper to Vinnie. "You can reach me at this number," she said.

He took the paper reluctantly and shoved it into the pocket of his baggy pants, without looking at it. He turned without a word and strode back down the hall, past the nurse's station, and Ben MacCready, who was still standing there watching, turned left into the far corridor and disappeared.

Ben came forward. "I guess you were right. He doesn't like you very much, does he?"

"What are you doing here?" Liz almost snapped it out, but she was too tired and weak to put much force behind it.

"Anytime anything happens to Vinnie Porelli or his son, I want to know about it. You never know. It just may mean trouble."

"You mean mob related?" Liz said. "Are you saying this wasn't an accident?"

"No. I'm not. I'm just saying that it's always a possibility when it's a Porelli."

"Does that go for me and my son, also?"

"Well Liz," he said. "You're not really a Porelli. And neither is James. If you know what I mean."

"Yeah, I guess so," she admitted. "Do you know what happened?"

"His car was found mangled to pieces with Michael inside. What ever hit him was pretty big. Whoever was driving, didn't stay around. Just left the scene. It was a back road without much traffic and it was a while before he was found.

That's all I know right now. Vinnie didn't want to talk to me either."

"Can't say as I blame him," Liz said softly, almost under her breath.

"What was that?" Ben cocked his head to hear, better.

"Oh, nothing," Liz said. "Just nothing."

"I heard you say you were staying in town," MacCready said. "Is Deb here with you?"

"No. She had to get back for work tomorrow. She just dropped me off here and I'll stay with a friend for the night."

"Is your friend picking you up here?" Mac-Cready asked.

"Yes. I need to call her and she'll come get me."

"No need to call her," MacCready said with a smile that Liz didn't quite like. "I can give you a lift if you like."

"No. No." Liz tried to mask the nervousness in her voice. She was suddenly remembering the things Deb had said about the police chief. Maybe Deb was right, she thought. "I mean, there's no need to trouble yourself. My friend won't mind. Really."

"No trouble at all," MacCready said with a smile as he grasped Liz's left arm near the elbow and started to turn her around.

Liz's pulse suddenly began to race. She felt the chill of fear wave over her, but she tried not to let it show that she was cringing from the man's touch. "Really..Ben, she stammered. "There... there's no need to trouble yourself."

"Nonsense," he said as he began to lead her back down the hallway toward the elevators. There was a force to his guidance and Liz felt like she might stumble, but she managed to increase her speed and keep up with the big man. "What are friends for if they can't help one another out," he said. He did seem to slow his pace, realizing that Liz couldn't keep up, but it was still a bit fast for her and she felt overpowered. She thought she noted a tinge of coldness in his words and his grip on her arm seemed to tighten. Just then, Liz seemed to lose her legs and they buckled under. MacCready did not miss a beat. He pulled Liz upright and steadied her on her feet. He said, "Sorry, Liz. We had better slow down, I just didn't realize. I've just been so used to rushing all my life."

Liz no longer protested. She just seemed to accept captivity with silence, while frightful thoughts raced through her brain. What if Deb was right about Ben MacCready? What if he had broken into her house? What if he did have some reason to harm her? No that can't be, Liz told herself. She had lived with Deb too long. She was now starting to believe her outlandish tales. That had to be it. Ben MacCready was her friend and the chief of police. He was one of the good guys. Or was he? What if Deb was right? No, that couldn't be. Or could it? Oh my goodness, Deb's going to say she knew I would think nice, nice of everyone, until they screwed me.

Chapter Twenty One

The night air had gotten even colder than it had been when Deb dropped Liz off at the hospital. Liz shivered and her body trembled. She felt wobbly even leaning on her cane. The wind had picked up and was whipping at her from the left. She pulled her coat collar up and held it tight about her neck, but the coat tails of her long winter coat flared up with the wind and the biting cold nipped at her legs through the thin fabric of her slacks.

She had been waiting for Ben MacCready to get his car from the ramp garage for less than five minutes, but the cold night air had made it seem longer than that as she stood just outside the front entrance to the hospital. As she wavered from side to side and back and forth against her cane, the automatic sliding glass door behind her would occasionally detect the movement and slide open and shut needlessly with the annoying sound of the activated motor mechanism.

She counted the cars emerging from the garage as the drivers stopped to pay the toll at the small kiosk. She had counted six cars already and each had driven off and turned into the drive leading down the hill from the hospital to the street below.

She didn't know what kind of car MacCready drove, but she knew he would have to swing to the left beyond the kiosk in order to circle around to the front entrance of the hospital to pick her up.

Two cars later, one turned in her direction, but she could see early on that it was not MacCready. The driver was an older man with long white hair. He pulled the car beyond where Liz was standing. A middle aged woman, who had been standing inside the glass wall enclosure, hurried out and got in the car. The car moved on, circled around in front of the kiosk and on down the drive toward the street, just as a black Chevrolet emerged from the garage and stopped at the kiosk.

The driver rolled down the window and leaned out to pay the attendant. Even in the dim light of the parking lot street lights, Liz could see it was MacCready.

Suddenly, her heart began to pound with fear, and she felt a pain in her stomach as her abdomen muscles tightened. A black Chevy! MacCready was driving a black Chevy. The man who had followed her and had stalked Celia Parks drove a black Chevy!

My God! Deb was right! Ben MacCready was a man to be feared after all! And she was going to be getting in a car with him. No! She couldn't do that. She would have to avoid it somehow.

MacCready took his change from the attendant and put it away in his wallet. He was lifting his body off the seat to put it away in his hip pocket as he let the vehicle roll forward past the uplifting gate.

Liz turned sharply and pushed herself through the automatically opening sliding glass door. She hurried through the inside door and across the lobby toward the hallway where the elevators were.

She stumbled as much as walked and used her cane only once every three or four steps. Her legs ached and her stomach pained with rising gas.

She reached the hallway and headed toward the elevators. She threw a quick glance over her shoulder and saw MacCready rushing in through the front door after her. She tried to hurry faster, but she was already doing the best she could.

What if she had to wait for the elevator? Mac-Cready would surely catch up to her. Chances were that he would catch her even before she reached the elevators. She made a quick decision. Forget about the elevators! A side hallway branched off to the right from the main one. She turned in here and headed for the next hallway that ran parallel. To the left it stretched toward the rear of the hospital. To the right it led a short distance back toward the front of the hos-pital and hooked to the left toward the Emergency Area. There were restrooms to the left side of this hall. First, was the men's room, and then the ladies'. She would hide there, if only she could get there before MacCready caught up to her.

Her legs just didn't seem to be working and were bending like rubber. It seemed to take forever to just pass the men's room. The ladies room seemed a long way off. What if MacCready saw her go in? What would she do then?

Panic and paranoia was engulfing her. What if she did get there in time? Would he be bold enough to go in the ladies' room looking for her?

Yes! He would! Of course he would! She needed a better place to hide and she spied a door next to her on the right. It had louvered slats high in the door for ventilation; obviously a storage or maintenance closet of some sort. And it was close. She wouldn't have to stumble any farther.

She tried the door handle and pulled. It came open and she smelled the mustiness of dirty mops and the pungent odor of disinfectant and detergent. It was a janitor's supply closet. She slid inside, pulling the door behind her just as she heard the clicking of rushing heels down the hallway from the direction she had just come from.

The contents of the stocked closet crowded her against the door. Her cane was pressed between her legs and was of no use to her. She held tight to the door handle and hoped she didn't make it move. She was breathing deeply now, but as she peered through the louvered openings she saw MacCready enter the hallway. She tried to hold her breath, but the pains in her stomach and abdomen were increasing in intensity.

MacCready looked up and down the hallway in both directions. Apparently, he decided she had not headed toward the rear of the hospital, because the hallway was too long and she would still be exposed if she had gone that way. He turned and headed toward where Liz was hiding.

Slowly, he moved forward; his dark eyes darting back and forth as he approached.

Liz sucked in a breath and held it. The pain in her stomach was excruciating now and she felt like she had to pass gas, but she held herself stiff and silent, save for the rumblings of her innards. She remembered the stories her little niece told of her friend, who passed gas for two minutes straight. She thought to herself, this could be her last thought on this earth.

He was almost directly in front of her now. He stopped in front of the closet, turned and glanced back the way he came. Then he turned back and moved on down the passageway to the ladies' room. He pushed the door open and shouted in. "Liz. Liz Porelli. Are you in there? He waited for a moment and then went on in.

Liz still holding herself in check waited until she saw him emerge from the rest room. His face was dark with anger and he stomped off back the way he had come.

As he disappeared around the corner, Liz let out a breath and let her taught body relax. But on so doing, she unleashed the monster as it took over her bowels and released the pent up gas. A stench filled the small closet and Liz felt the momentary warmness between her legs before it turned to a cold sticky wetness streaming down her pant legs.

She clenched her eyes tight shut with despair as she realized what was happening. Of all times for this to happen, when she was alone, in danger, and far from home without Deb to help her, clean up after her, and say funny, snippy things to make her more comfortable and take it all less personal. After all, this was the monster, not her. She leaned her head against the door and started to sob, but after a moment she took hold of herself. Tears were not going help her. She was going to have to get a hold of herself and do something. She couldn't stay in this closet. And she was going to have to clean herself up, somehow, some where.

Ben MacCready had already checked the ladies' room, so perhaps it would be safe to go in there now. It would have to be, Liz told herself. The only thing she could do now was to get in there and out of her soiled clothes and clean herself up.

Slowly, she pushed the closet door open, looking up and down the hallway in both directions. No one was in sight. She pushed her cane out in front of her and realized that it was also soiled. Her fingers slipped on the gooey brown covered handled and her hand came away with the same material smeared on it. She re gripped it and leaned forward on it, walking slowly toward the ladies' room door. Her legs were bowed and she tried to hold them away from the stickiness between her legs. Her slacks sagged with the weight of the mess and she felt the sliminess continue to trickle down her leg. She tried to hold her coat out from her body to keep it from becoming infected. Her right shoe was already covered as was the sock around her ankle. A brownish tread mark was left in the middle of the hall.

Her odor followed her like a cloud and it seemed like it took forever to reach the ladies room.

Once inside, she opened a door to a stall, pulled off her coat and held it up to examine it. It didn't look like it had been stained. She hung it on the stall door hook and went to work at stepping out of her shoes and peeling off her slacks and socks and underwear that were pasted tight against her skin. She cleaned herself up as good as possible with toilet paper, then, proceeded to the sink to wash off her cane and shoes. At first she was going to try to wash her clothes in the sink, but decided against it. The clothes were too soaked and stained. There was no time to try to salvage them. Besides she had nothing to carry the wet clothes in anyhow, even if she could get them clean. She wrapped them in paper toweling and stuffed them in the waste paper receptacle. She then washed up as good a possible and dried herself. Oh, how she wished she could shower; she felt so dirty. Her legs and bottom half of her body felt clammy and the wet shoes felt cold and rough on her sockless feet.

She put on her long coat, over her naked body, and buttoned all of the buttons and left the ladies room. When she emerged, there was no sign of MacCready or anyone else for that matter, in the hallway. She continued on down the corridor toward the front of the hospital and into the lobby. Still there was no sign of MacCready. Perhaps he had given up and left, she hoped. She headed for the front entrance once again. But now, she felt like people were looking at her and knew she was naked, beneath her coat.

As Liz stepped through the open sliding glass door, she once again felt the wrath of the cold night and the strong wind. This time it felt even colder as the chill blew up under the coat and attacked her naked flesh. She lifted her cane so she could hold both hands against her coat to hold it tighter to her body.

Just as she did this, she froze with a start. The black Chevy was still in the circle. Ben Mac-Cready was still there!

She half turned to look back inside the hospital lobby. At the far end, just emerging from the main corridor near the elevators, she could see him entering the lobby.

Her heart was racing once again and she felt so tired. She tried to move away from the door, but her legs felt like lead and she was sure she was not moving. But she was moving and everything was rushing past her in a blur and slow motion at the same time.

She felt herself bumping up against a wooden wall and then realized that she had moved far enough away from the main entrance and past the parked Chevy to collide with the green wooden fencing that surrounded the Emergency Room expansion construction site. Her fingers slid along the wood as she traced her way to the front corner of the enclosure. She thought to herself, that if she ever got home again, she was never going to leave it again.

She turned around and looked back. Mac-Cready was just coming through the entrance door. She twisted around sharply; her back to the wall and rolled around the corner into the shadow of the sidewall. She pressed her back tightly to the wooden slats and caught her breath. She rested a moment, wondering if MacCready had seen her. Needing to know, even though not wanting to know, she peered out around the corner. She saw MacCready standing in the light of the entranceway, looking about.

Liz pushed herself back around the corner, once again pressing her back to the wall. The wind whipped through her hair and she felt naked with the wind rushing up beneath her coat. It made her think of Marilyn Monroe in 'Some Like it Hot', when she walked over a grate in New York City, which was a blow off from a factory and her dress flew up over her face. Only, this time the air was biting cold and the force of it pulled the lower buttons of the coat free. She slipped back into the shadows, hoping Mac-Cready didn't come this way. She was feeling weaker by the moment and only through sheer will power did she manage to move. She slid her back along the wall, using it for support; dropping her cane somewhere along the way.

She had reached the far end of the wall when she saw the lights of MacCready's car flash into the drive, heading down to the street below. If he were to look to the left as he passed by, he might see her there against the fence. She rolled around the corner to the back wall into further shadows. As she twisted, her foot slipped on the wet grass and before she could realize that the back wall ran along the top of a hill above the street below, she found herself falling. The ground came up hard and she rolled down the bank all the way to the sidewalk at the bottom of the hill. A streetlight glowed above her as she lay there unconscious; her coat flung open and hiked above her waist, leaving her lying there; bottom half naked to the world.

Chapter Twenty Two

Meanwhile, across town, it had been another boring, uneventful day for Celia Parks. She had just moped around her apartment all day. She tried to watch television for a while, but she found nothing to interest her. As much as she tried to divert her thoughts, she kept thinking about her suspension and the problems at the hospital. Maybe it had been all her fault after all and she had made a mistake. A fatal mistake.

From time to time, she would get up from the couch and pace the floor, occasionally looking out the living room window, seeing the same scene before her.

In the corner of her mind she kept remembering the black car and the man who had sat outside that one night. She would stand for several minutes and carefully scan the traffic and the parked cars in the neighborhood, but each time she saw nothing out of the ordinary, especially the black car. It had been only one time and it probably didn't mean anything. In her wrought up state, she was probably jumping at shadows as she had told herself a million times.

The clock ticked past eleven when she finally decided to give up on the day. She flicked the TV off. She wasn't even aware of what was on or even if the current show was beginning or ending. She decided to shower and get ready for bed. Perhaps she could finally go to sleep and pass some hours.

By a little after midnight, she was finally ready for bed, dressed in her flannel pj's. She went around the apartment and shut each light off. Only the light from the street outside provided what light was still left in the apartment. It was just enough for Celia to see her way around.

She walked to the living room picture window and reached for the cord to draw the drapes. She had them half drawn when she halted with a start. Parked on the street below, was the same black car she had seen before. It was back. This time there was no man inside it. Where was he?

She yanked on the cord hard and the drapes flew together with a snap. She whirled around and jumped away from the window as if it was alive.

The doorbell buzzed and she jerked her head toward the door. It suddenly looked a long way off as if she was looking at it through a distorted haze. She jumped back toward the window, her back hugging the wall next to it. A dull throb pounded in her head. She waited silently, staring at the door. The door bell buzzed again.

It's him, she thought. He's come for me. But why? What have I done?

She watched the door. She could see the door knob turning on the inside. Whoever was out there, was trying the door. She had a dead bolt. The knob stopped turning. Whoever was out there, now knew he couldn't get in. There was no way he could get in, she told herself. She would wait. Keep still. Maybe he would go away. She could call the police. They could send someone out to protect her.

She waited for what seemed like an eternity; listening and watching the door, until she was pretty sure she heard nothing more outside her door, she ventured forward across the room. She crept silently up to the door and put her eye to the peep hole. There was nothing out there. Just an empty hallway. She breathed a sigh of relief and darted toward the phone on the coffee table.

She had gone about two and a half steps, when she froze in her tracks. There was a fist pounding on the door. She whirled around to face the door. The rapping sounded again. This time it sounded more urgent. She backed up toward the coffee table, bending and reaching for the phone. It was time to call the police. She didn't care if the man outside heard her. Her fingers had just curled around the receiver handle and she was lifting it from its cradle, when the knocking sounded again. This time a voice came with it.

"Ms. Parks? Are you all right? Open up! This is the police."

It was a deep voice and it had a mellow ring to it. It sounded far from threatening. Had someone called the police? That must be it. But what if this was just a trick to get her to open the door? She must be careful.

She slipped quietly back to the door, leaned against it and listened as the voice sounded again. "We're here to help you Ms. Parks. Open the door."

If she answered the man, for sure he would know she was inside. But then again, he already knew that. She forced herself to speak. "How do I know you're the police?" Her voice was weak and cracking.

"Look through the peep hole," the voice answered.

Celia slid her cheek along the side of the door and pressed her eye to the little aperture. There it was directly in front of her. A policeman's badge held in a large hand. She couldn't see the man behind it.

"All right," Celia said meekly as she slipped the dead bolt free and opened the door.

As she stepped back inside her apartment, Ben MacCready stepped into the open doorway, took a step toward her and closed the door behind him.

Vera Porelli rolled over on her back and reached for the phone on the nightstand next to her bed. She was still half asleep, not sure what was happening, but somehow she automatically was responding to the ringing phone without really knowing what she was doing. But by the time she put the receiver to her ear, she was starting to come out of her slumber. "Yeah, what d'ya want?" She mumbled through a yawn.

The voice came on and she suddenly snapped awake. She sat upright and propped the pillow behind her. "Yes. Sure," she said into the mouthpiece. "I'll get him." An urgency was now in her voice and she was fully awake. She shook her husband's shoulder and he merely rolled away with a mumble. She shook him harder and he fought her off, hugging his pillow.

"Jim. Jim. Wake up," she shouted. "It's Frank Porelli. Something's happened to your mother."

Jim Porelli rolled quickly away from his pillow, lurching up into a sitting position and grabbing the phone. "What is it, Frank? What's happened?" He was wide awake.

"She's all right now," Father Frank Porelli said at the other end of the line. "She's here in Buffalo."

"Buffalo? What's she doing in Buffalo? Isn't Deb with her?"

"No, she isn't. It's a long story. Your mother wants you to come get her. She'll tell you all about it when you get here."

"Sure. Sure," Jim said rising from the bed, looking for his pants. "As soon as I get dressed, I'll be right there." He started to put the phone away, but he heard Frank say, "Jim. I need to tell you where to pick her up."

"What? Isn't she there with you?"

"Well, yes. But, we're not at my place." He sounded reluctant to tell the whole truth.

"Then where the hell are you?"

Father Frank stammered a bit. "We're at the jail. Your mother's been arrested."

"Arrested," Jim Porelli boomed. "What the hell for?"

There was a pause at the other end of the line. Frank said, "For.. for flashing, Jim. For flashing."

"Flashing what?" Jim asked. Then the picture came to his mind. He paused. A long pregnant pause. Then said, "No way! No! You can't possibly mean that kind of flashing."

Chapter Twenty Four

"Jesus, Mom," James Porelli fumed. "What the hell were you thinking? Getting arrested for flashing." He shoved his foot angrily against the accelerator and sent his Camaro faster into the darkness ahead. "You've done some real stupid things before, but this beats all. When word of this gets out, I'm gonna be the laughing stock of the town council. Hell, I might not get re elected next year."

Liz was too tired to listen. She slouched back in the passenger seat and let her throbbing head rest against the back rest. Flashes of street lights waved over her periodically, as the car rolled on. She closed her eyes to keep them out, but she could still tell when they passed by. James' voice was ringing in her ears with an echoing din. She wished she could just turn a switch and turn him off.

Finally, she could no longer stand his ranting and she opened her eyes, pushed herself more erect in the seat and said, "For crying out loud,

Jim. Can't you shut up? I told you what happened. I wasn't flashing and it was all a mistake. They wouldn't have let me go if it wasn't." She was still wearing the orange prisoner trousers she had been issued in jail.

"That's not the point, Mom," James said. "It doesn't matter if it was a mistake or not. The fact is you were arrested for it and that's all anyone is going to remember."

"Well, you don't have to tell anyone about it."

"What do you think will happen when you start spouting all that nonsense about Ben MacCready? He's the Chief of Police, for Christ sakes."

"It's not nonsense. It's true. Deb knows it too. But, I wouldn't believe her."

"Never believe anything Deb says. That's your problem, Mom. You've been living with that fruit cake much too long."

"Deb takes good care of me. I don't see you coming around to help."

"Now don't start that again. You know I have other commitments. I just don't have the time."

"Besides, Vera wouldn't like it either." Liz added for him.

"Now, just wait a minute, Mom. This has nothing to do with me or Vera. I'm talking about you and what happened tonight."

"That's what I'm talking about too. What happened tonight. It was a nightmare for me and all you care about is you. If it had been up to me, I would've called Hal to pick me up. Francis just assumed you were the one to call, since I told him not to call Deb."

"Fine. Excuse me for coming to your rescue." James pouted.

"Look, Jimmy," Liz said as she did when he was a little boy. "I appreciate you coming for me like this. In the middle of the night and cold as it is, but I just don't want to listen to your constant bantering. I have had too rough a night and I'm tired. Can't you just let it go until tomorrow?" She slouched back in the seat and closed her eyes. James glanced at her, knowing she was shutting him out now. Maybe she was right, but he sure as hell wouldn't apologize to her.

It was afternoon when Liz woke up. There was a heavy weight on her chest and as she opened one eye to a slit, she saw big brown eyes staring into her face. Sissy Boom Boom had crawled up on her bed and lay across her, staring into her face waiting for her to wake up.

Sissy raised her head as she saw Liz's eyes start to open. She wagged her tail and licked at Liz's cheek. Liz put her hands around the little pug and pushed her back from her face so the tongue couldn't reach it. She rubbed the pooch affectionately behind her ears and said, "Oh, poor baby. Mommy's left you alone for so long hasn't she?"

Sissy rolled over on her back. Liz raised herself to a sitting position and rubbed the little dog's tummy. She smiled at Sissy as she played. Suddenly, a darkness came over Liz's face as she remembered the night before. It had been almost like one of her terrible dreams, but her sleep had been dreamless, which was a rare occasion for Liz. The night before had been real and still vivid in her memory, unlike the fleeting memory of a bad dream.

She picked up the pooch and hugged her, holding her tight against her. She looked about the room and listened to the silence. Deb had gone to work and she was all alone. Fear started to creep over her. What if MacCready came after her while she was here alone? She had better get up she told herself. She would call Hal to come stay with her.

When James had brought her home the night before, Deb had awakened briefly to help Liz into bed. Liz had not told Deb what had happened, for she didn't want her to think she had to stay home from work to protect her. Besides, she didn't feel like going into the whole story, any how. She had just wanted to get to bed.

She put the pooch down and shooed her onto the floor. She swung her legs over the side of the bed and reached for her cane. It wasn't there. Then she remembered she had dropped it outside the hospital. That meant for sure, the night before had been real.

"What do you think, we ought to do now?" Hal Hall asked. He was sitting on the couch across from Liz. She was holding Sissy Boom Boom on her lap and rubbing her behind the ears.

"I don't know," Liz said. I'm afraid, but I don't think anybody is going to believe me about Ben MacCready."

"No," Hal said emphatically. "They won't. You're not going to like this Liz. But I find it hard to believe myself." Liz started to say something, but Hal added. "It's not that I don't believe you, Liz, but I know Ben, and I just can't believe he's what you say he is. Maybe you've just jumped to the wrong conclusions."

Liz shook her head vehemently. "I know what happened. He chased me. He's followed me and stalked Celia Parks. It couldn't be any clearer than that. What other conclusion could I come to."

"I don't know," Hal said. "But, there's got to be some explanation to all of this."

"But, there isn't any, Hal."

"Maybe we should talk to Tom about this. He might know something," Hal suggested.

"I thought about that," Liz said. "But, I didn't want to call the police station. I was afraid Ben would be there and know I was home."

"He probably does anyways," Hal said. "I can't see him not checking on that, the first thing back here."

"Then why hasn't he been around. If he meant to harm me last night, why didn't he follow me home and finish the job?"

"I don't know, but maybe you answered your own question."

Liz looked perplexed. "What do you mean by that?"

"Just maybe, he didn't mean to harm you after all."

Liz thought that over for a moment. Absent-mindedly, she put Sissy down and reached for the candy dish on the coffee table. The little pug scampered away into the kitchen as Liz plucked a lollipop from the dish and unwrapped it. Cherry. She put it in her mouth, tasting it and pushing it to the side so it made a bulge in her left cheek. "How about you call Tom for me. Maybe he can come over."

Hal took out his cell and started to dial. "I thought you'd never ask," he said.

The phone rang on the other end and a female voice came on. "Sadie," Hal said. "This is Hal Hall. Is my son Tom there? I'd like to talk to him."

"No, I'm sorry. Tom is out on a case. But, Ben's here, and he'd like to talk to you. Just a minute while I put him on."

Chapter Twenty Five

Mondays were always bad for James Porelli, but this one was worse. Not only was the monthly town meeting scheduled for tonight, but it was Halloween besides. It had rained earlier during the day and the streets were still wet. The night glare of street lights and car headlights always made it hard to see at nights. The little goblins dashing in and out of the street as they went on their way for trick or treat made the driving even more frustrating. Twice already James had to brake for the little buggers and he cursed them out to himself inside the privacy of his car.

He was nervous about the meeting tonight, even though it had been a few days since his mother had humiliated him. So, far no one had mentioned anything to him, indicating that it had become public knowledge. But, he did not feel at ease that the incident had gone unnoticed. He expected Ben MacCready to have told the story by now, but he hadn't. Why not? James wondered. Perhaps, MacCready didn't know about it either. He also wondered how his mother was doing and more importantly if she had said any-thing to anyone. Especially about MacCready. If she had that would certainly let it all out of the bag.

He was already late for the council meeting, when he pulled into the parking lot next to the town hall. It was already ten after eight and the Mayor was always prompt about bringing the meeting to order at exactly eight o'clock. Oh, how he wished he didn't have to go in there. If only he could turn around and go home. But, he supposed, that would just mean postponing the inevitable. There was nothing else for him to do, but get out of the car, put one foot ahead of the other and walk inside.

"Nice of you to make it, Councilman," Mayor Gridly said as James came in through the side door. The Mayor was a plump little man, with a round face and jowls hanging down like mutton chops. His voice was gravelly and caustic.

"Sorry for being so late, Mister Mayor," James said as he hurried in and passed in front of the long table that had been set up on a platform at the far end of the room. There were a half dozen townsmen sitting in the gallery.

James took his usual seat at the table with the other three council members. Ted Beasely, the high school principal sat to his left and Martin Callan sat to his right. The Mayor had the center position and his Town Clerk, Maggie Summers, sat next to him on the other side with Lew Drum to her right. Sue Blaine, the secretary sat at the far end of the table.

"Now that Councilman Porelli has graced us with his presence, I suppose we can proceed now," Gridley said sarcastically.

James seemed to shrink into his chair and his shoulders rounded. He kept his head down, his eyes staring at the table. The Mayor went on with the business at hand. James found it difficult to concentrate on what was going on and the Mayor's raspy voice merely echoed dully in his ears.

The usual mundane details of the meeting went on with the reading of the minutes from the last meeting and the offering of the latest financial report before Jim finally composed himself enough to concentrate on the business at hand.

For a small town, participation from the gallery was usually small, and tonight was no exception. Of the half dozen spectators, only two had anything to present. One was complaining about dogs running about town unleashed. Another complained that garbage pick up was too early and she liked to sleep in.

By a quarter to nine, four of the spectators had left and the meeting was winding down, when the rear door opened.

James jumped erect in his chair as his mother and Hal Hall entered. Liz shuffled forward leaning on the new quad cane she had just purchased. Hal steadied her on the left as they made their way to the front row and seated themselves.

James' eyes met those of his mother's. He saw that determined look that always made him shudder, ever since he was a little boy. He knew that when his mother was set on doing something, there would be no stopping her. And he was sure he knew what she was here for. He quickly looked away from her and slumped back down in his chair. If only he could be invisible.

From here on, he could barely listen. The dread was just too heavy on his shoulders, but somehow he could hear the mayor recognizing her and giving her the floor to speak.

"Mister Mayor, Distinguished Council Members, I come before you with a matter of grave proportions," Liz said, trying to sound like a Turner Classic Movie actor in a courtroom drama.

James shook his head with despair. Then suddenly, he pushed his chair back and stood up, "Mister Mayor," he interrupted. Gridley's round head bobbed. His beady eyes flared with annoyance. "Before Mrs. Porelli presents the issue," James continued. "I suggest we take her concerns up post meeting after all participants have left."

"Sit down, Councilman," the mayor barked. "You are out of order. And must I remind you that this is a public forum open to all citizens. We have nothing to hide from the public." He smiled his oily politician smile at the two remaining people in the gallery.

"Perhaps, Mister Mayor," Liz started again with a less stilted form of speech. "Councilman Porelli is right. I would feel more comfortable without an audience."

"All right," Gridley growled. "But these proceedings will be recorded and available for the public at a future date. Is that understood?" He glared at James and nodded to Liz.

Liz nodded in return. The gavel sounded and Gridley ordered. "The gallery will now be closed except for Mrs. Porelli."

"Now, Liz," Mayor Gridley said quietly. His demeanor was friendlier and less formal now that they had adjourned the formal meeting. They had moved to the conference room across the hall where everyone could sit around the large oval table. The door had been closed and locked. "What is this matter that's on your mind."

"Well, Fred," she started to say with comfort, then remembered herself. "I mean, Mr. Mayor," she quickly corrected herself.

"We've been friends a long time, Liz. It's okay to call me Fred as long as we're not in an official meeting setting."

Liz smiled, pulled a handful of lollipops out of her coat pocket and tossed them in the center of the big table. "Help yourselves, gentlemen; and…ladies," she added as an after thought.

She picked one up herself and unwrapped it. Cherry. Things were still going good.

The mayor picked one up but the others refrained.

"Well, this may shock you, but I assure you it's all true," Liz started.

"Mother," James butted in; a feverish tone rising in his voice. "You don't have to do this. Why don't you just go home and give it a rest."

Liz ignored him and looked directly at the mayor. "It's important that I report this," Liz started to say again.

"Mother. Don't do this. Please." James begged.

"That'll be enough of that, Jimmy," Gridley chided like a father. "Your mother is old enough to know what she's doing. And, obviously she thinks it's important to bring to our attention." Then his tone became more accusatory and grim. "And more obviously, young man, you know what this is all about and you haven't already brought it to our attention. I find myself quite perplexed that you would keep something important from the rest of us."

Then to Liz, he said in a much more congenial tone. "Now, Liz. Why don't you continue with what you have to say." He glanced at James and his tone was stern. "And there will be no further interruption from the council." He turned back to Liz with a smile and nodded for her to proceed.

"What I have to say here, is about Ben Mac-Cready, our Chief of Police," Liz started. James hung his head and sighed; dread permeating his entire body. He shook his head in despair.

Liz went on to tell about MacCready's stalkings of herself and Celia Parks. She told of her suspicions about him being the intruder that had broken into her house and about he had tried to abduct her from Amity Hospital.

The mayor and the council listened intently as she went on. The expressions of disbelief and perplexity was common to them all. When Liz had finished, there was complete silence in the room for several moments. Finally, Fred Gridley spoke up. His gravelly voice was low and heavy with concern. "Liz," the mayor said. "I've known you a long time and I know you are not one to make things up or exaggerate them, but I've known Ben MacCready a long time too and he has been a good Police Chief. He has been known to be honest and forthright. He has an excellent high standing in this community. So, please don't take offense that I find these allegations to be beyond my belief." Several of the board members nodded their agreement.

Liz's eyes flared with a bit of anger. "It's all true......," she started to protest, but the mayor held up his hand in a halting motion and interrupted.

"Just wait a minute, Liz. Hear me out. I do believe that you believe it is all true. I'm merely saying that perhaps, you've misinterpreted these things and perhaps there is some reasonable explanation that may put his actions in a different light."

"I've tried to think otherwise," Liz said. "I couldn't believe it myself at first. But then as everything happened, I had no other explanation. I had to believe it to be true."

"If it is," Gridley said. "What reason would he have for this kind of behavior."

"I don't know," Liz said. "Perhaps he had something to do with what happened to Joe. Maybe he hurt Joe, just to get his job."

"I find that hard to believe, also," the mayor said. "That hardly seems like a motive." Then to the council members, he said, "Any comments from the council."

The members looked from one to another, each waiting to see if the other had something to say. After a moment, Martin Callan spoke up. "I agree that it's hard to believe that Ben Mac-Cready could be guilty of anything sinister, but we should all remember that none of us really knows anyone else that well. Who knows what any of us are capable of. I don't think Liz would come to us crying wolf or making things up, but as I say, none of us knows anyone else that well. I think we should bring these allegations before Ben MacCready and give him a chance to defend himself, if he can. If we find that what Liz believes is true, we should bring him to justice, just like we would anyone else. Probably more so. Afterall, he is public servant and we have entrusted him with the safety of our community and if that trust has been violated, he should be made to pay for it."

The response around the table was non existent. Callan looked from one member to another, waiting for agreement. James Porelli was still staring down at the table. Lew Drum caught Martin's glance and quickly turned his face away. Beasely was nodding affirmatively, weakly. The Mayor stared at Callan warily. "Don't you all agree?" Callan asked finally, requesting a direct response.

Beasely spoke up his agreement and there was a slight unenthusiastic grunt of agreement from Lew Drum.

"I hate to believe anything bad about our Police Chief," the mayor said. "But I guess I have to agree with you, Martin. We need to confront Ben MacCready. I suggest we call a special meeting, closed to the public of course and confront him with these accusations." Then to Liz he said. "I think it only right, Liz, that you be here and re-state what you have just told us. Ben has a right to face his accuser directly."

The car heater was just starting to warm up. Liz and Hal had left the meeting ahead of the others and had been sitting in the car for ten minutes. From their vantage point, parked along the side street that ran parallel to City Hall, they could watch the members leave the building one by one, save for the Town Clerk and the Secretary who came out with the mayor first. The mayor walked across the parking lot, got in his car and drove away. The two women had obviously ridden to the meeting together as they both got in the same car and left. The school principal was the next to leave. Then Martin Callan followed by Lew Drum.

Liz and Hal watched from the darkness until the last car left. Hal turned to Liz and said, "Well. What do you think?"

Liz took the lollipop from her mouth and said, "I think it's time to fasten your seat belt, it's going to be a bumpy ride."

Chapter Twenty Six

"I don't think a return to the steroids would help any at all," Roger Callan said as he came into his office and took his place behind his desk. Liz was sitting in the chair at front of his desk. Her examination had been completed in the other room and she had been waiting here in his office for a couple of minutes. The clock on the wall said two thirty seven.

"They did help before," Liz argued. "I just thought that since I wasn't feeling any better, that perhaps I should try them again. Lord knows I haven't been feeling well since that last medication you put me on. Actually with all that's been going on lately, I missed the medication several times and quite frankly, I felt better when I didn't take it and felt terrible every time I got back onto it. If I didn't know better, Roger, I might even think you were trying to make me sick with that stuff."

Roger Callan's face turned gray and he stared coldly at Liz. Then she said in a lilting tone. "Don't take me serious, Roger," she said apologetically. "I'm just talking. I didn't mean to accuse you. I know you have my best interest at heart. I trust you."

Roger forced a smile, but the palor of his face denied it. "Oh, I know that Liz. No offense taken."

Liz took a pop out of her hand bag and offered it. It was obvious that Roger wanted to refuse, but he took it any ways and laid it aside.

"You realize, of course, that a steroid treatment would require the infusion process again. I know you never liked that and I'm not sure, in light of what happened last time, I could get you in until the investigation is over. Perhaps we would have to try a different hospital."

"Oh, no," Liz seemed to blurt it out. "That wouldn't do." Then she seemed to catch herself, trying to lessen the concern in her voice. "I...I mean, I really would prefer to go to Amity." She wrung her hands nervously.

Roger eyed her warily. After a moment, he leaned back in his chair, twirling his pencil with both hands near his chest. "All right,Liz," he said flatly. Calculating coldness was in his eyes and his brow deepened. "Perhaps we should try it again." He abruptly stood up in dismissal. "I'll call Doctor Blakeney and have it set up."

Liz was gone but a moment, when Roger Callan strode to his door and closed it. He quickly returned to his chair behind the desk, picked up the phone receiver and dialed quickly. He squirmed nervously in his chair as he waited, listening to the ringing on the other end of the line.

It was ten to four when Hal Hall wheeled his Volkswagen into a parking spot outside Celia Parks' apartment building. There were two consecutive spots there and with the little car, he didn't need to parallell park. He could merely drive in.

Just inside the vestibule to the right was the stairwell. The first flight stopped at a landing then twisted to the left for another flight. Liz cast a wary glance from the stairs to Hal. He knew what she was thinking. No way was she going to climb those stairs. He glanced around beneath the stairs and spotted a small elevator door set into the wall.

"This way," he said as he guided around the stairs toward the elevator. Liz felt a bit relieved.

Moments later, they stepped off the elevator and walked a short distance to the left and stopped in front of Celia Parks' door. Hal pressed the doorbell button and they could both hear a buzzer like sound on the other side of the door. They waited for a few seconds and when there didn't seem to be any sound of activity from inside, Liz glanced impatiently at Hal, reached over in front of him and leaned on the buzzer. A sense of urgency welled up inside her and suddenly she felt that there might be something wrong. She removed her finger from the button, balled her fist and started pounding on the door.

She staggered and almost fell forward as the door suddenly opened inward, her arm was still raised and her fist was pounding empty air. Celia grasped her by the wrist to hold her up. Surprise was on her face and she said, "Liz! Are you all right?"

"Yeah, I'm all right," Liz answered. "The question is, are you all right?"

"Why, yes. Of Course. Why wouldn't I be?"
"No reason," Liz said straightening herself. "Of course you're all right. Why wouldn't you be?" She gazed over Celia's left shoulder and saw Ben MacCready standing in the living room behind her.

"Hello, Liz. Hal," the police chief flashed a smile. The ends of his bushy black mustache turned slightly upwards. "I got here early."

Celia closed the apartment door behind them as Liz and Hal made their way into the living room. Ben sat back down in the overstuffed chair he had been sitting in. Hal took the chair opposite him while Celia and Liz sat on the couch.

"You've already been to the hospital, then?" Liz asked as she settled herself as comfortably as she could. She preferred a chair to a couch, but she didn't complain.

"Yes. And I'm pleased to say that Michael is much better. He was able to tell me what actually happened the other day. I have to admit that I thought, myself, that he had been hit deliberately by a cement truck, just to persuade him to keep off Arnold Pruitt's back, but it turns out that it was nothing more than an accident after all. He had been sideswiped by a tractor trailer and the driver kept going. We've managed to track the man down. Turns out he's a new driver. Just a kid. He was on his second run and was afraid he'd lose his job if he stopped and reported the accident."

"Then there was no attempt on Mike's life after all. We were just jumping at shadows then?" Liz said.

"We might better jump at shadows than to miss something lurking in the dark," Ben said. Then he changed the subject. "So how are you today, Liz?" He said. "You look even more tired than you did the other day."

"I've missed my nap today. That's all. But I'll be all right." She took a few lollipops from her coat pocket and held them out in an offer. No one accepted so she kept one out and put the others back. "I'm actually much better than when you saw me the other day."

The day after Liz's ordeal at the hospital and her arrest for flashing, Hal had called the police station looking for his son, Tom, hoping for help against MacCready. Hal was surprised to find that Ben MacCready, himself had wanted to talk to him and Liz. He had assured them that he meant no harm to either of them and if they would meet with him, he could explain about a lot of things that had been happening of late. He offered to meet them in a public place, if that would be more agreeable to them.

Liz and Hal finally agreed to meet with him at the thruway rest stop in Depew. Over coffee in a booth at the back of McDonald's, MacCready explained that after Liz's disappearance at the hospital, he had been concerned about her and had gone to Celia Parks' apartment hoping to find her there. He had given Celia quite a scare for she thought he was a stalker. She had recognized his black Chevy that he had driven following Celia and Liz to Vinnie Porelli's car dealership and then followed her home and watched her building for several hours.

He had explained how he had seen Celia's car parked in front of Liz's house that first day he had gone to question her. When he had left Liz, the car was still there. Afraid that someone was stalking Liz, he had gone back to the police station, retrieved his own personal car and returned to keep watch. When Liz and Celia came out of the house, got in her car and drove away, he followed. He had recognized Celia as an attendant at the hospital where Liz had had the infusion and wondered what she was up to, so he followed her home.

"How did you know who she was?" Liz had asked him.

Ben seemed a bit hesitant to explain, but knew he had to in order to gain Liz and Hal's trust. He just wasn't quite sure how he should start it.

"I had been shown pictures of her." He paused. The others waited expectantly. "You see there was someone else at the hospital who worked with Celia that was not really who she thought she was." He leveled his gaze at Liz.

A quizzical expression clouded Liz's face. Ben continued on before she could utter a question.

"A month or so, ago," Ben said. "I was approached by a young lady who told me she was a free lance journalist. She was working on a story about terrorists and money laundering."

"What would that have to do with Celia?" Liz interjected.

"Nothing," Ben said reassuringly. "She just happened to be one of the people she met."

"Who….. who is she?" Liz asked.

Ben took a deep breath, let it out and said, "Shirley Robbins."

"Shirley Robbins!" Liz and Hal both said in unison.

"But she's a medical attendant." Liz said.

"Not really. As I said, she was a journalist. She got a job as a medical attendant just to get close to Doctor Blakeney."

"What does he have to do with anything?" Liz asked.

"Plenty," Ben answered. "He's a link in a chain helping people channel ill gotten money into legitimate enterprises for the sole purpose of hiding the source of that money and redistributing it back in the form of new less recognizable funds."

"Money laundering, you called it," Liz said.

"Yes. A lot of money flows through oil and gas and pharmaceutical companies as investments. Blakeney, using his position at the hospital he has contacts with several pharmaceutical companies." He looked straight at Liz. "One of those companies produces the experimental drug you were given through infusion."

"Does that mean.....?" Liz started to say, but Ben cut in.

"We don't know if that means anything about what happened to you and the Pruitt woman. All we know is that money had been funneled through Blakeney and a lot of money had its origin from right here in Mandalyn. That's why Shirley had come to me. She had asked my help in finding out who, in our town could have access to that kind of money."

"So that's why you were out with her. I saw a picture of you in a photo album and Deb and I thought..."

"And Deb thought I was out cheating on my wife," Ben completed.

"Well yes. It did look suspicious and.....Hey! Wait a minute. Deb said you have the album. How did you get it?"

"I'm sorry. Liz, but I was still wondering what was going on and I was still following you the day you took it back to that lady. After you left her, I went to the door and asked what you were doing there. She rambled on something about the album that I didn't understand, so I confiscated it.

I took it back to the office but didn't find anything interesting about it." He turned to Hal. "It was Tom who found the picture with me and Shirley in the background. In light of what had happened earlier in the week, I decided to keep it under wraps. I didn't want anyone questioning me about knowing Shirley."

"I don't understand," Liz said.

"Because Shirley Robbins is dead."

There was complete silence at the table for a moment or two.

"You see," MacCready continued. "The girl killed in a car accident a while back was Shirley Robbins. And I don't think it was an accident. The car went over the bank all right, but I think she was dead before it happened. I think the car had been deliberately pushed."

"You think someone from around here did it?" Liz asked, her voice seeming small.

"Yes. I do," MacCready said emphatically. "Shirley had left me a voicemail on my cell that night that she was afraid she was being followed. You see she had been at the hospital late at night and had found documents that would blow the case wide open."

"She knew who from Mandalyn was involved then.?" Liz said.

"I think so. She didn't say and she never got the chance to tell me. There were no documents in the car when we found her."

"Do you have any suspicions as to who it was?" Hal said.

Ben sighed heavily. "Yes, I do."

Now several days later there in Celia Parks' apartment they were meeting again. "Has there been any fallout since the town meeting?" Liz asked

Ben chuckled to himself. "Yes. There has been. The Mayor and Martin Callan came to see me yesterday." He glanced at Liz and smiled. "Seems you did a good job at the meeting. I wasn't sure whether it whether Lew Drum was in on the money laundering scheme or not. Him being the town banker and all. He certainly could have access to large amounts of money. I never did understand how he was able to open his own bank and make a go of it. I did hear that he had come into some money through an inheritance. I know his first wife had money."

"But now you think it's Martin Callan for sure," Liz put in.

"Yes," Ben said. "He certainly seemed eager to make an issue out of your complaint. Looks like our plan worked. I figured that whichever one of them was involved would see this as an opportunity to move me out of the way."

"Well, I'm glad it wasn't Lew," Liz said. "After all that has been happening to that man. I wouldn't want to see him have more problems." Then she said, "But where did Martin get all that money?"

"I don't know," Ben said. "He had some money that his father left him, but I know it wasn't much. That old stone quarry that his father owned had been closed for years before he died, so there couldn't have been much left."

"I didn't know his father owned the stone quarry," Liz mused. "You mean the same one that Joe was found beaten up in."

"Yes. That's right," MacCready caught himself and changed his tone. "Hey, now wait a minute. Don't start jumping ahead of ourselves and start speculating that Callan had anything to do with what happened to Joe."

"Where did the money come from to start the farm equipment dealership and send Roger to college and medical school? That never occurred to me before," Liz said.

"I don't know," Ben answered. "But if it had been gotten legitimately, there would be no reason to launder it."

"So what are you going to do now?" Hal asked.

MacCready looked Hal straight in the face and said grimly. "The only thing we can do is continue with the plan."

Hal looked from MacCready to Liz and back. His face was pale with concern.

"I know it's putting Liz in danger, Hal. But Liz is willing to do it. I promise I'll be on it all the way."

"If you can," Hal said grimly. "What happens if you can't."

"Let's try to not think about that for now," Ben said, then turned to Liz.

"Did you make the appointment with Blakeney."

"Roger is going to take care of it. He'll call me when he has it set."

"Would someone mind telling me what is going on here?" Celia piped up.

"Ben and I thought we would try to unnerve Doctor Blakeney. Maybe make someone else nervous. I went to my doctor today and asked for another infusion process. He didn't think it was a good idea, but I told him I wanted it anyhow."

"How is that going to help?"

"Ben thought if I could meet with Blakeney, I might hint that I know something about what's going on at the hospital. It might rattle him enough to contact Callan, if it really is him."

"I just hope it doesn't push them into harming Liz," Hal said. "She's already had a couple of attempts on her life. If they killed the Robbins girl, what would prevent them from killing again?"

"We don't know if those incidents had anything to do with this," MacCready came back. "Somehow those things just don't seem to fit."

Chapter Twenty Seven

"I wish I hadn't told you about this, Deb. I should've known you'd get all hissy about it. Mac knows what he's doing and I'm going along with it." Liz was sitting in her usual chair in the living room. Sissy Boom Boom was on her lap and relishing the petting she was getting.

"So, now its back to being Mac, again, is it?" Deb snorted. "Just the other day, you were scared to death of him."

"Well not that scared." Liz protested.
"Not that scared huh? Scared enough to fill your bloomers, that's all."

"That was just the M.S. You know that happens every so often. Besides, so what if I was scared of him then. I'm not now. He explained everything to me."

"And you believe him. Any man that would sneak around his wife's back with that Sadie woman…."

"You don't know that for sure, Deb. Why don't you just give it a rest."

"Sure, sure. I'll give a rest. The next time Ben MacCready breaks in here don't expect me to keep him from strangling you."

"Why on earth would he ever do that? We all know that the intruder was probably the same one that had been breaking into other houses and killed poor Marlee."

"If that's the case, what's your precious Mac doing about that?" Deb emphasized the word 'Mac'.

"I don't know," Liz confessed with a half pout. "But I'm sure he's working on that too."

Deb started to say something, but was interrupted by the phone ringing. She picked up the handheld from the end table and snapped gruffly. "Hello. Whadaya want."

When the voice on the other end sounded, her face brightened. The fire from her eyes disappeared and the corners of her mouth curled upward. "Oh, Hello Mikey," she said in the sweetest of tones. Deb was like a radio that could change stations instantly. "How're you doing sweetie?" She said. "I wanted to come see you, but your old man don't like Liz on account she has a big mouth."

Liz clenched her teeth together. He don't like you either, Deb, she thought to herself. Big mouth. She should talk.

"Yeah. Well sure, Mikey," she heard Deb say. "I'll give her right over to you." She handed the phone over to Liz and made a face.

"Hello, Mike. How are you?"

"Fine, Liz," Mike answered. "Sorry about my dad keeping you away."

"No. No, that's all right," Liz said apologetically, then, thought how that must sound. "I mean, I just wanted to know you were okay."

"Well I am," Mike said. "I should be out of here in a few days."

"I'm sorry Mike. This was all my fault. I never should have pulled you into this mess."

"Nothing's your fault, Liz. Besides, it was just an accident. Pure and simple. It had nothing to do with my snooping around."

"You're a good boy, Mike."

He disregarded the 'good boy' and said, "I did find out that Pruitt had financing from Lew Drum's bank and Lew knew Pruitt's wife."

Liz was silent for a moment; a bit surprised. "I..I don't know what you're getting at, Mike. Are you saying that Lew Drum is mixed up in this too?"

"I don't know," Mike answered. "It's just that, Pruitt's wife put up collateral for a loan, so Lew had to have known them both. It's just a connection, though. I know of no other involvement. But, apparently Lew never told you that he knew her."

"Maybe he didn't know she was the one who died on my medication."

"It was in all the papers. But, I suppose, maybe he didn't read about it. Did he ever talk to you about it? Or you to him?"

"Now that you mention it, no. I did talk to Marlee about it, though." She paused then said,

"But Mike, I'm sure Lew had nothing to do with any of this. The poor man has enough troubles of his own."

"I'm sure you're you right, Liz," Mike said, not sounding convinced. "I just thought I'd run it by you. And I did want to talk to you. I hope you're doing all right."

"Oh, I'm fine, thanks." She didn't want to tell him about her ordeal at the hospital and her subsequent arrest.

"Good," Mike said. "I'll let you go for now. I am a bit tired. I'll keep in touch."

"Thanks Mike."

"Bye for now," Mike said. "I'll call again." He hung up.

"Bye," Liz said softly to the dial tone. She clicked the phone off and handed it back to Deb. Deb placed it in the cradle and stared expectantly at Liz.

After a moment or two, when no news was forthcoming, Deb said, "Well, what's up?"

"I don't know," Liz said quietly and half to herself; thinking. "I just don't know." Then she shook Sissy awake and put her on the floor. The little pug shook herself off. "I guess it's time I went to bed." Liz said.

Deb had already gone to work, by the time Liz got up the next morning. She had awakened surprisingly refreshed for a change and couldn't recall any bad dreams from the night before.

She had poured herself some coffee that Deb had put on before leaving. No matter how put out with Liz that Deb could get, she always continued to take care of her. This morning was no exception and the coffee was as good as ever.

Liz lingered over her coffee, thinking deeply about all of the recent events. There were so many things going on, she was totally confused. Lew Drum, Martin Callan, Shirley Robbins, the recent breakins, and Marlee Drum's murder. Were they all connected in some gigantic puzzle or were they all separate incidents? It all seemed so jumbled, just like the M.S. itself, with its bits of scar tissue breaking logical thought into bits and pieces of related and unrelated thoughts. Perhaps the reality of life was no different than Multiple Sclerosis; just random acts and incidences that have nothing to do with anything. Maybe nothing really makes sense anyhow.

The phone rang before she had finished her first cup of coffee. It was from Roger Callan's office. The girl had called to tell Liz that the doctor couldn't get her an appointment with Blakeney or anyone else at the hospital until the investigation of what happened before was done. In the meantime, if Liz still wanted the steroid infusion, she would have to go to the hospital in Rochester.

Liz didn't know what to say, but dared not refuse, so she agreed to it. Immediately upon hanging up, she called Ben MacCready and told him what had happened.

"I was afraid that might be the case," Ben said. "But, hopefully, we've started to make someone a little nervous."

"What do we do now?" Liz asked.

"I don't know. Just don't worry about it. I'll come up with something else. Just hang tight and I'll get back to you." He hung up.

Liz didn't like that. She wasn't ready to hang up yet and she felt that MacCready had brushed her off a little too quickly.

She was beginning to feel jittery. It couldn't be the coffee, she thought, but she pushed the half empty cup aside anyways. She just didn't feel comfortable sitting tight as MacCready put it. She had to do something. Talk to someone. She picked up the phone again, checked her directory and dialed the bank.

"No. Lew hasn't come in yet today," the girl at the other end of the line said. "Do you want him to call you when he comes in?"

"No. No. That's all right. It's nothing urgent. I'll call him another time." She hung up.

No sooner had she put the phone down, it rang.

"Hello."

"Liz, it's me, Deb. Hey, I want to know, if Martin Callan is a bad guy, do we gotta give the tractor back?"

"Oh, for heaven's sakes, Deb. Is that all you're calling about? And is there anybody around you that could hear you? What I told you about Martin Callan is not to be repeated. If it gets out that he's suspected of anything, it'll ruin everything. I knew I should've told you to keep your trap shut about this."

"Well excuse me for not having any brains, dearie. Of course I'm not letting anything out of the bag. How stupid can you be?"

"How stupid do you want me to be?" Liz answered with a classic Lou Costello line.

"Ha. Ha. Very funny, dearie. I'll tell you one thing, I know who's on first. Gotta go." She hung up.

"Oh, Deb," Liz said to herself as she clicked the phone off and put it down. "For once in your life, please don't say or do anything stupid."

It had been quite some time since Liz had driven the Cherokee. Today she felt she was strong enough to tackle the job. She had gotten nowhere by phone today and she needed to do something.

It was colder outside than what Liz had expected, for the sun was shining, but there was a slight wind and the air was bitter with cold. As she drove into the center of downtown, the heater was just starting to kick in. That was the problem with short trips, you were never able to get warm before you got where you were going. But Liz didn't know where she was going, she told herself without admitting that she was hoping to catch Lew Drum at the bank when he came in.

"Would you like some more coffee, Ma'am?" Deb said to the blond haired woman in the center booth next to the front window. She held the coffee pot in her hand.

The woman considered it a moment, then said, "Sure. I guess I have time." She smiled coldly as if forcing it. Crows feet crinkled at the corners of her eyes and lines appeared on her brow, despite all the makeup, and belying her attempt to appear more youthful than her approaching middle age.

"That's what I like to hear, dearie," Deb said as she poured the coffee. "Always good to stop and smell the roses." She wrinkled her nose as she joked. "Or should I say 'the coffee.' Ain't none of us gettin' any younger."

Deb was laughing at her own joke, not realizing that the woman might not like the crack about getting old, but the woman seemed to pay no attention.

Deb was still basking in the euphoria of her own little joke, when suddenly, her face turned grim. The corners of her mouth turned downward and she set her jaw.

"What the hell..?" She said aloud to herself. She pulled the coffee pot quickly back from the cup, not noticing that she almost spilled some it. "What's she doing?" She was still asking herself as she gazed through the plate glass window at the passing traffic.

Liz had just driven by in the Cherokee. She tried to tell herself she was mistaken, but as the vehicle passed by, she checked the license plate.

It was Liz all right and she was up to something without telling Deb.

It could mean only one thing, Deb told herself, without saying it aloud. She put the coffee pot on the table and headed for the door. On a coat and hat rack next to it, she retrieved her motorcycle jacket and helmet. "Hey, Morris," she shouted to the small oriental man behind the counter. "I gotta go. I'll be back."

She had the door open and was on her way out, when her boss, Morris Wong shouted. "Hey. You can't do that. It'll be lunchtime soon."

"Don't worry. I'll be back." The door slammed behind her.

Liz turned the Cherokee into the parking lot at the back of the bank. She noted right away that Lew Drum's car was parked in his reserved spot. She drove on past and found three empty parking spots in a row. Good, she thought. Her parking skills may not be so good anymore. She wheeled into the middle spot, parking diagonally across it with her left rear wheel overlapping the line to her left and the front right wheel overlapping the line to her right.

She turned the engine off, swung the door wide open and reached for her cane. She was just placing the bottom of her cane on the pavement and hanging onto the metal hand rest she had had installed to help her slide down from the seat. Her left leg was hanging half way to the ground when a black and white police car rolled into the parking lot and stopped almost, but not quite behind her.

Ben MacCready rolled down his window and said, "Liz. What in the world are you doing out here? And on your own? Should you even be driving?" He shut off his engine as he spoke and got out of the car.

"You want to see my driver's license, Officer?" Liz said sarcastically with annoyance.

MacCready ignored the attitude. "What's going on Liz?" He said with concern.

"I don't know, Mac," Liz said shaking her head. "I just needed to do something. I just couldn't sit around doing nothing."

"And.....?" MacCready waited.

"I wanted to talk to Lew. That's all."

"What about?"

"Do I have to tell you everything? Is it any of your business?"

"Probably, if you're messing around in an investigation. Then, yes. You do have to tell me everything."

"Well, if you must know, Michael told me that Lew knew the Pruitt woman. You know the one that died at the hospital when my infusion bag was switched. I just wanted to talk to Lew and find out if he knew that's who it was. He never said anything to me about it."

"And you wanted to know if he was deliberately hiding something?"

"Not really." She didn't seem to be convincing herself. "But I just wanted to be sure."

"I understand," Ben said. "Michael told me too. He asked me to check into it. That's why I'm here." Then he added, "And I'm glad I got here when I did. I don't think you should be here. Now if you are up to it, I think you should go on home. But if you're not absolutely sure you can drive back by yourself, I'll drive you. I can always come back later. I'll see that the Cherokee gets delivered back to you."

"Really, Ben, I'm not helpless. I've got M.S., I'm not dead. Of course I can drive myself. I got here didn't I?"

Ben nodded. "I just don't want you to be a danger to anyone on the highway. It's my job."

"Well, go do your job and I'll take care of myself. She turned herself in the seat to sit square behind the steering wheel and brought her cane up and passed it to the passenger side. She slammed the door as hard as she could, to show her irritation.

MacCready grimaced. Liz started her engine and shifted into gear. MacCready jumped back into his car and drove forward, just barely out of her way as she applied the gas with a heavy foot and shot the Cherokee backward across the spot where Ben had been parked and halfway across the parking lot. She cranked the wheel. Shifted into drive and squealed the tires as she peeled forward and shot out into the street, turning left and cutting off another car from her right that had to brake suddenly to a screeching halt.

Ben MacCready shook his head with exasperation as he watched her go in the reflection of his rear view mirror.

Deb hardly throttled down the engine of her red Honda as she turned off the highway into the parking lot of Martin Callan's farm equipment dealership. She whipped the handle bars sharply to the left and slid the bike sideways to a halt infront of the entrance.

In one smooth motion, she had turned off the ignition, shoved the kick stand down, leaped off the machine and darted inside, without first checking the lot to see if the Cherokee was in fact there in the parking lot.

For a small person, she took long quick strides through the showroom and was within a few feet of Callan's office in a matter of seconds. As she approached, she saw the four bottom prongs of a quad cane protruding into the doorway, its length angled up toward the visitor's chair in front of Callan's desk and just out of sight from the doorway.

"Liz," She shouted excitedly as she practically slid to a halt in the doorway. "You can't do this............" She cut it off in mid sentence. Martin Callan was staring up at her with surprise. There was an elderly man sitting in the vistor's chair. He was portly with gray hair and bushy gray mustache. His hands were clamped over the top of his cane. Through the thick lenses of his wire rim glasses, he also stared at her; a stunned expression on his face.

Deb froze in place. For once in her life she was speechless. Her eyes darted back and forth from one man to the other. Her eyes widened and she murmured, "Uh…oh," under her breath to herself.

"Deb," Callan said sharply after a moment of composure. "What's going on here? What's the meaning of this?"

"I……uh. I……," she stammered. "Uh….I dunno. Uh…. I mean…..I dunno." She was still glancing from one man to the other. Then as if suddenly recovering from the shock of her mistake, she tried to cover things over by saying. "I… just thought Liz was here and I wanted to stop her."

"Stop her? Stop her from what?"

"Uh.. I dunno. I mean, she was going to send the tractor back. And I still want it?"

"Send it back? Is there something wrong with it?"

"No. No. It's fine. It's…it's just that she thinks we shouldn't spend that much money after all."

"She told me, she could afford it," Callan said.

"Oh…yeah..sure. She can afford it. She's got lots of money. Only….only she doesn't…., can't use it just yet." Deb felt like she was blubbering incoherently, and she was. This sounds so lame and stupid, she thought to herself.

"Can't use it?" Callan exclaimed. He glanced at his customer who still looked very confused.

A wary expression spread over Callan's face and his eyes darkened. He pushed himself to his feet and said to his customer, "If you will excuse me for a moment Mr. Boggs. I'll be right back."

He came around the desk and grasped Deb by the arm, practically pushing her backward through the doorway. "Let's talk about this, Deb," he said sternly as he guided her away from the doorway.

His grasp was hard and Deb's arm hurt from the pressure. She saw the rising anger in him and the hard set of his jaw. Somehow, Deb no longer felt like the spitfire she often pretended to be. In light of what Liz had told her about Martin Callan, she was genuinely scared.

When he had ushered her into another office and shut the door, he released his grasp on her so suddenly and forcefully that she stumbled backward a step, bracing herself against the front edge of a desk which prevented her from falling.

"Now what are you talking about?" Callan demanded. "What's all this about money she can't use."

"Well... it's like this." She was stalling; trying to think fast. What to say? Then it occurred to her and she said. "She's got money, Joe gave to her a long time back. Before his accident." She tried not to emphasize the word accident, knowing full well it was not. "He put it where she can't touch it."

"Why was that?"

Deb could see that she had really piqued his interest now. Maybe she was onto something. "I don't know," she said. "Maybe he just wanted it to last for her."

"I don't think I quite understand you." There was a sharpness to his voice and his eyes had a grim menace to them.

"I..I really don't know anything else. Really I don't." She was arching her back over the desktop now as if trying to move farther away. Her eyes were wide and round.

"Deb," Callan said softening his voice and taking a different tact. "Are you afraid of me?"

"No. No. Why should I be afraid of you?"

"Well, you are acting awfully strange." He stepped back a little to appear less threatening.

"Uh… caffeine buzz," she blurted. "Too much coffee. I keep drinking the bottom of the pot. At the restaurant you know. Before I make a new brew."

"I really do think you ought to cut back a little." He forced a smile.

Deb tried to force a smile back, but couldn't.

"I take it Liz doesn't know you're here?" Callan said.

"No. No. Just like I told you. I thought she was already here and I came to stop her."

"Should we call her now?" Callan suggested.

"Gosh, no. I wouldn't want her to know I came here and made such a fool out of myself." She straightened herself, becoming a little less stressed. "I just wanted to keep her from sending the tractor back. You won't tell her will you?"

"Trust me," Callan said flatly. "I wouldn't dream of it."

Chapter Twenty Eight

Liz was still agitated as she maneuvered the Cherokee down Main Street, heading for home, where she really did not want to go. She still felt at loose ends, and unable to settle down. She was driving the vehicle below the speed zone limit and just putting along. She was always a careful driver and had been more so as the M.S. had progressed. She didn't feel reckless nor did she like driving that way. What she had done at the bank was strictly for Ben MacCready's benefit and to demonstrate her anger.

It had been bothering her all morning that she had told Deb everything that was happening and she wasn't sure just how reliable Deb could be about keeping it all under wraps. Usually, the best way to spread news around town would be to tell Deb, and she would take it from there. As Liz approached the Gossip Grill, coming up on her left, she made a decision. She put on her left signal and pulled close to the center line in the street. She came to a stop in front of the drive that led to the back of the restaurant. She let two cars from the other direction go by, then twisted the wheel sharply, floored the gas pedal, and shot across the street, bouncing into the drive before the next oncoming car would get too close.

She rolled to the back parking lot and found a parking spot way in the back where the employees usually parked. She noted that Deb's Honda was missing from her usual spot. She glanced at her watch. It was only ten fifteen. Still a few hours from lunch time. Besides, Deb usually worked through the lunch hours and she should be on the job. A dread crept over Liz. What was Deb up to? Whatever it was, Liz was pretty sure that it couldn't be good.

She decided she would still go inside. Perhaps, Morris could tell her where Deb was. She turned off the engine and started to open the door, when she heard the familiar sputter of Deb's Honda approaching. Liz pulled the door shut and rolled down her window.

"Good Morning, Sunshine," Liz called. Deb had parked two spaces down from where Liz was parked. She had just turned off her engine and was dismounting, not noticing the presence of the Cherokee.

She looked a bit chagrined as her ears recognized the voice and she slowly turned her head to see Liz.

Liz was smiling smugly and crooked her index finger toward Deb.

Deb muttered something to herself under her breath and walked over to the Cherokee. She was taking off her helmet and shaking out her hair as she tucked the helmet under her arm.

"Where've you been?" Liz demanded.

"Well, where've you been?"

"I asked you first," Liz said.

"Okay. Then I guess it's your turn to answer first."

"I went to see......" Liz started to say. Then she caught herself. Deb was doing it again. She always had a way of turning things around. "Hey, wait a minute. That's none of your never mind. Where've you been?"

"Well, I guess that is kinda my never mind and it's none of your never mind, neither."

"Deb you can be so exasperating at times. I got a half a mind........"

"That's right. You only got a half a mind." Deb cut her off.

Liz ignored it and started to repeat, "I got a half a mind to..........." Her words trailed off again. "Hey who's that?" She lifted her chin as if pointing toward the restaurant.

Deb turned and looked behind her. She saw the blond haired woman she had been waiting on earlier. "I don't know. Just some old broad who's trying to tell herself she's still a hot young chick. I hate to tell her, but it ain't workin'. She comes in for coffee and a little something a couple of times a week. Why?"

"She looks familiar. That's all." The woman had walked around the rear of a dark green Saturn and was fishing her keys out of her purse. "At first I thought…but it couldn't be. It wouldn't make sense." Liz paused. "Then again, maybe it does. Quick! Get in. You're driving." She pushed the driver's side door wide open, and started to slide across to the passenger seat.

"What for?" Deb exclaimed, hardly moving.

"Never mind. Just get in and drive."

The woman had her car door open now and she was sliding in behind the wheel.

"For heaven's sake, Deb. For once in your life will you do what you're told and just get in, before she gets away?"

Deb hurried and climbed into the cab, pulled the door shut behind her, turned the ignition and kicked the engine into life.

The woman had already backed her Saturn out of the parking spot and was cranking her wheel to turn toward the open drive.

"Will you just move it, Deb?" Liz shouted again, her voice shrilling with panic.

Deb was maneuvering the Cherokee as rapidly as she could and muttering under her breath, her jaw hanging low. "Where we going?" she shouted back as she pawed at the wheel.

"Just follow that car!"

"Well, why didn't you say so in the first place." Deb's face brightened suddenly. "Just like TV, huh?"

"Yeah, Deb. Just like TV. But hurry up. We don't want to lose her."

Deb tromped on the gas and shot toward the street. The Saturn had already pulled out and turned right. The Cherokee bounced out into the street with tires squealing. A car from the other direction braked to a sudden halt and almost slid into the Cherokee's rear bumper.

The Cherokee fish tailed a bit, then, straightened out as Deb floored the gas pedal. The Saturn was far down the street by now. Deb leaned over the steering wheel as if willing the vehicle to go faster. She was going too fast to slow down when she saw a car coming out of the bank parking lot and entering the street ahead of them. Deb stood on the brake, shoving it as far down as fast as she could, but the momentum was too great. The Cherokee slid forward, tread from the tires painting marks on the pavement and the stench of hot rubber filled the air.

Deb's arms went rigid against the steering wheel, pushing her back against the seat upright behind her. Liz pushed her arms out in front of her and braced herself against the dash.

It all happened so fast, that it seemed like flashes of light and color before her eyes. She screamed without hearing herself, or Deb next to her. Only the crash and the sound of metal against metal registered in her brain.

In an instant it was all over. Liz bounced backward against the seat, her neck snapping backward and sending pain up and down her spine. The monster now took the opportunity to take charge of Liz's body. Her vision blurred and she had no control over body movement.

Next to her, Deb was trying to fight her way through the bulky remnants of the inflated air bag that pinned her between the seat and the steering wheel. The driver's side door came open and a man's voice said, "Liz. Are you all right?" With the Cherokee up against the dented in driver's side door of the black and white, Ben MacCready had slid across the seat and had gotten out on the passenger side. His left hip hurt a bit from the impact of the crash.

Then as Deb fought her way out of the air bag, MacCready said with surprise, "Deb. Where did you come from? I thought Liz was driving......" His gaze spread to the passenger seat. Liz was sitting straight back; her eyes glazed and staring blankly forward. She was catatonic.

"I should arrest the both of you," Ben Mac-Cready said. He was sitting in Liz's usual chair in her living room. Sissy Boom Boom lay in her chair and eyed the big policeman warily. Deb was sitting on the couch and looking very gloomy. She didn't bother to give MacCready any of her usual back talk.

She had just put Liz to bed and had given her medication. Liz was sleeping soundly now.

"But I don't suppose that would do any good," Ben sighed. "So why don't you just tell me what the hell has been going on this morning?"

Without any of her usual attitude, Deb told him about Liz recognizing the woman who drove away in the Saturn and how Liz had insisted that they follow her.

"Did Liz tell you who she thought the woman was and why she wanted to follow her?"

"No. She just told me to get in the Cherokee and drive. So I did."

"And just where had you been before you met up with Liz in the diner parking lot?"

"You promise you won't tell Liz if I tell you?" Deb was reluctant, but still subdued.

"That depends," MacCready said. "If I don't have to tell her, I won't. But I can't promise. You'll just have to trust me."

Deb lifted her head and leveled her gaze at Ben MacCready. She swallowed hard and said feebly, "Okay."

Deb told him that Liz had told her about Martin Callan and how she didn't really believe it until she went to Callan's place thinking she could head Liz off from turning the tractor back. She told Ben how Callan had frightened her and had been rough. She told how interested that Callan was in Liz's money and how his attitude had suddenly changed.

MacCready listened intently, his mind methodically putting pieces together. When Deb had finished, MacCready gave her a reassuring smile and said, "You did just fine, Deb. I don't think I have to arrest you after all."

Deb brightened, "Really?"

MacCready chuckled. "Really. But I still have to give you a ticket."

Deb's face began to darken again. MacCready said, "Just kidding." He smiled broadly.

"Oh Ben, thank you," she beamed proudly.

Chapter Twenty Nine

Liz was up a nine the next morning. Deb had already left for work. She had left a note saying that Morris Wong had fired her for leaving so abruptly, but as usual she would report to work and Morris would take her back as he did every other time he had fired her.

Liz's neck and her back hurt like the devil and her vision was still a bit blurred, but she could at least move and get around, although she had to relegate herself to a wheelchair for the day.

She had had a fitful night's sleep and she had awakened exhausted. Her dreams had been muddled with random flashes of light and darkness permeating her brain with occasional flashes of an intruder approaching her bed in the middle of the night and of a crumpled body in a pool of blood on a living room floor.

There were children in Halloween costumes in her doorway shouting trick or treat and a witch's pale white skeletal face rising above the throng of children with arms extended and hands with long spindly fingers and sharp nails reaching for her throat.

Then she was running naked through a dark city street with good legs that needed no assistance from a cane. Then she had a rain coat flapping open around her. She tried to pull her coat together and zip it up, but the zipper was stuck. Joe came staggering out of the dark; his head a bloody mess. He disappeared and Scooby Doo danced in front of her eyes.

Then darkness moved in and deep sleep settled over her until she awoke with the morning sun streaming through her bedroom window.

Now as she wheeled herself to the counter where coffee was brewing, she was thinking about calling Celia Parks. She poured her coffee and started to drink it without wheeling to the kitchen table.

She sipped at the hot brew. It was still too hot and it tasted bitter. Liz knew it was her and not the coffee. Deb knew how to brew coffee perfectly. She set the cup on the counter, then turned her chair and rolled into the living room. Sissy Boom Boom raised her head from her pillow and waged her tail as Liz came near her.

Liz retrieved the handheld from the coffee table and punched in Celia's number.

The phone rang several times, before a sleepy voice sounded from the other end.

"Celia? This is Liz. Did I wake you?"

"No. No. I was just waking up. Just lying there trying to decide if it was worth getting up."

"Listen, Celia. At the hospital, there was a nurse there. You knew her last name but you weren't sure about the first."

"Yes. I only knew her by her name tag. It said N. Taylor. I just assumed it might be Nancy, but Michael talked to her and he said her name was Natalie. Why?"

"I think I saw her right here in Mandalyn," Liz said.

"What would she be doing there?"

"I don't know, but I'm going to find out. Thanks a bunch." She pressed the hang up button, excitedly. Then she punched in another number and listened for the ringing at the other end. Ben MacCready came on.

"Mac? This is Liz. I've got something to tell you."

"And I've got something to tell you too."

"Hello, Martin?" Liz asked even though she recognized Callan's voice when he answered. "This is Liz Porelli."

"Yes Liz. How are you?"

Liz ignored the niceties of polite greetings. "Martin. Deb told me all about yesterday. I need to talk to you alone." Without pausing she continued. "Deb won't be here tonight. Could you come over?"

"Sure Liz," he said in his most pleasant voice. "I'll be glad to." He didn't even bother to ask what it was all about. He smiled smugly to himself as he hung up.

It was dark when Martin Callan showed up at Liz's house. She greeted him cordially and invited him in and ushered him to a chair in the living room. She was well enough now to be using her cane.

Sissy Boom Boom growled lowly in her throat and jumped out of her chair, scampering off to the kitchen. Liz sat down across from him. "Deb told you about my problem," Liz said getting straight to the point.

"You mean about the money?" He asked carefully.

"Yes. I understand you can help me." Liz stared expectantly into his eyes.

He fidgeted, "Why do you say that?"

Liz ignored the question. "I think it's time that I use that money."

"You know where Joe got it, then?" He sounded a bit skeptical but there was a trace of excitement rising in his voice.

"Of course, I do. Joe told me everything." She kept her tone level, trying to hide any trace of uneasiness or fear.

Callan's face turned gray. This was just what he had been afraid of.

"You know where he got it, too. You've always been questioning me about my finances."

The gray in Callan's cheeks turned to red as anger began to rise. "Yes," he almost growled it out. "And I want it back." He stood up and towered over her. Liz tried not to tremble.

"That's not possible," Liz said flatly.

"Oh, yes it is. If you want to go on living."

"So," Liz said. "It was you all along trying to kill me. First at the hospital and then breaking in. I suppose you broke into Lew Drum's house and killed Marlee too. Just to make it look good."

"Oh, no," Callan sneered. "I didn't have anything to do with those breakins. I didn't kill Marlee Drum and I didn't have anything to do with what happened at the hospital."

"I know about you and Doctor Blakeney," Liz said, pushing it just a bit.

"Yeah, you may know about that, but that doesn't mean that either of us had anything to do with that woman's death. You might want to ask your friend about that. Everything got screwed up when that bitch of his put poison in the bag."

"Poison? So how do you know that?"

"They found traces of it in the bag. We couldn't have a murder investigation going on, so Blakeney covered it up."

"Why did anyone want to poison me?"

"You dumb broad," Callan chided. "I thought you knew something here. It wasn't meant for you in the first place." Then he changed his tone. "Now are you going to give me my money back or do you become another victim of an intruder?"

Liz had lost her composure by now and she was trembling. She felt dizzy and her vision was blurring. "Deb told you, I can't get to it."

"What do you mean? I thought you just couldn't use it."

"That's right. I can't."

"Well then where is it?"

"In a trust fund. I've told you that before."

Callan clenched his fists with rage. "What the hell do you mean a trust fund? Why the hell do you need to launder it then.?"

"I didn't say that's what I wanted to do."

"Then what the hell did you call me over here for?"

"To find out for sure, that's what you and Blakeney were doing. From what you're saying I guess it is true. Isn't it?"

"Yes, but I don't know how you found it out. Who else knows about it?"

"Well, you know I wouldn't tell Deb. For sure everyone would know about it by now."

"In that case, then," Martin Callan moved closer, raising his huge hands reaching for Liz's throat. "M.S. isn't going to bother you anymore."

"Before you do it, Martin," Liz said in a shaky voice. "I just want to tell you where Joe got the money."

"Like I said. I know that. He stole it from me." His fingers were curling around her throat. Liz shivered and wriggle in her chair; her body sinking into the plush back of her overstuffed chair.

"No he didn't!" Her voice was raspy as the fingers tightened. "He won it off a horse called Vivatar."

Callan's grasp relaxed a bit, then he went at her with more strength. "You bitch," he growled.

Liz's eyelids closed and she began to choke. Her mouth came open and her tongue tried to escape over her teeth. A man's voice sounded muffled in her ears.

"Let her go, Martin!"

Callan leaned back, slackening his grip some as he looked over his shoulder and saw Ben MacCready standing in the hallway; his Gloch police pistol thrust forward with two hands and his feet braced in a shooting stance. He had been in Liz's bedroom listening. Waiting for the right moment to show himself.

"Let her go, or I'll shoot you dead, where you stand." The Police Chief repeated. His eyes were glaring.

Callan released his grip, straightened up and stepped away from Liz, raising his hands. Liz was rubbing her throat and her voice was raspy. She chided, "Why didn't you wait a little longer, Ben? He just might've finished the job."

"Just wanted to give him enough a chance to spill everything," Ben said. Then to Callan he said, "You want to tell us about Shirley Robbins, now?"

"Tell you what?" Callan sneered. "I'm not telling you anything until I talk to my attorney. My lips are zipped. You can't prove a thing."

All zipped up Liz thought to herself as she listened to MacCready read Callan his rights. She should have thought about it before. Perhaps she had, without realizing it, for somehow she had realized it. She had noticed it. She remembered her dream of the night before. The raincoat with the broken zipper.

Chapter Thirty

Lew Drum was busy with a customer so he didn't see them at first, when they came in.

It was a sunny day for November and sunlight streamed in through the bank's front window. Ben MacCready held the door politely open while Liz stepped through into the lobby. They could see Lew Drum in his office at the rear of the bank and kitty corner from the teller's cages. There was a slim elderly woman sitting in the visitor's chair in front of Drum's desk. She had her long winter coat still buttoned tight around her and her round shoulders were hunched over the desk. Lew was pointing out something to her on a paper before them.

The banker seemed to freeze in place for a moment as he caught a glimpse of the newcomers. He stared past his customer and watched The Police Chief and Liz approach.

They were halfway to his office when Lew stood up from behind his desk, gathering up the papers. The woman stood up and the Banker ushered her quickly out of his office. Peeking into the next doorway, he said, "Marilyn. Will you take care of Mrs. Trask?" He ushered the woman into the office, putting the papers on Marilyn's desk and motioning Mrs. Trask to sit down, without waiting for an acceptance from Marilyn.

He turned and stepped back to his own doorway waiting for Ben and Liz. His usual ruddy complexion paled, but he forced a smile. "I take it, you're here to see me," Lew said trying to keep his voice calm. He could feel his knees shaking. "Good morning, Liz," he acknowledged.

"That's right, Lew," Ben said flatly.

Lew stepped aside and motioned for them to step into his office. Liz glanced from Lew to MacCready and said, "If you don't mind, Mac. I'd like to talk to Lew alone, first."

MacReady nodded and stepped back to allow Liz to enter the office.

Lew Drum looked away from the police chief and kept his eyes down as he followed Liz into his office. Liz was already seating herself in the visitor's chair when Lew swung the door shut behind them. Through the glass in the upper part of the door, he could see Ben MacCready seating himself in one of the waiting chairs in the hallway.

"I told Ben yesterday that I didn't realize that Jane Pruitt was the lady that died from your medication in the hospital," he said as he moved around behind his desk and sat down. He was trying to control the quiver in his voice.

"Yes," Liz said. "He told me all about that."

"Is there something else, then?" He acted as if he wanted to know what was going on, but he feared deep down in his soul what might be coming and he really didn't want to know.

"We just thought you might want to know that Martin Callan was arrested last night."

"What on earth for?" Lew exclaimed, not having to feign surprise.

"Seems he was involved in a money laundering scam with someone at the hospital. Last night, he tried to kill me. He was going to take advantage of the recent break ins and make it look like I was killed by an intruder."

"Just like Marlee? You mean he's been staging these things, just to get at you. You mean he killed my Marlee just to get at you?"

Lew relaxed a bit. Maybe it was all right after all. "But why? Why did he want to kill you? What possible reason could he have for it?" Then he said, "And are you saying he was behind that attempt on your life in the hospital too?"

"No, Lew," Liz said shaking her head. "I'm not." She stared directly into Drum's dark eyes. Drum stiffened, waiting. Liz continued. "Buffalo police have also arrested Natalie Taylor." Drum's chest sank and his head bowed. He could no longer look at Liz. His shoulders were shaking now, though it didn't show through the thick fabric of his suit coat.

"She's admitted to putting poison in the bag to kill Jane Pruitt. The bags weren't switched at all. She merely switched the name tags afterward to make it look like the bags had been switched. Need I say more, Lew?"

He raised his head, placed his arms out in front of him on the desk and clasped his hands. "I was against it from the start. I told her..." He looked back down toward his hands and the desktop. "But how did they find out about her?"

"I saw her here in town, Lew."

"I told her it was a mistake to come here, but she insisted that there was no one here, who could identify her. Oh, I knew you might possibly be able to, but you're not usually about in town in the early morning or late at night." He shook his head with despair. "The trouble with that woman is she would never listen to me. I told her that it wasn't necessary to kill Jane, but I think she just wanted to get even with her anyhow. You see, I met Jane when I did some business with her husband some time back. We..we had a relationship for awhile. Then I met Natalie when I was taking Marlee in for treatments. Things got a little out of hand between us and eventually I broke things off with Jane. She was angry with me and threatened to tell Marlee about Natalie. She even went so far as to send her an anonymous note."

"Marlee showed it to me, Lew. She had faith in you and didn't really believe there was anything to it. She thought it was just a cruel prank. At least that's what she wanted to think." Then she added in a subdued voice, "So did I, Lew. So did I."

The banker jerked his head up, feeling the disappointment in Liz's voice. Tears were starting to form in the corners of his eyes. He fought hard to keep his composure. "Believe me, Liz. I didn't think Natalie would really do it."

"So why was Jane Pruitt getting the infusion anyways?" Liz asked.

"She had been checking up on me. She wanted to get to Natalie so she arranged for the B-12 treatment just so she could meet her."

"Sounds like she wasn't a very stable woman, then?"

Lew shook his head. "No. She was a very mean, vindictive woman."

"But at least, she didn't kill anyone."

Drum sat back with a start.

"Seems to me you haven't been picking very nice women at all. That is, with the exception of Marlee. She was a nice lady."

"She was," Lew said. "She didn't deserve to have me cheating on her. It was tearing me apart what I was doing to her. I was going to break things off with Natalie and try to make things up to Marlee, but she was killed before I had a chance to."

Liz was silent for several moments. She stared at Lew Drum. Her face was placid and her eyes began to water also. She shook her head despairingly and said, "It's no use, Lew. I know you killed Marlee yourself."

"Wh...what...what are you saying," he stammered nervously. "That's ridiculous. You know yourself that I didn't do it. You were with me at the nursing home at the time. You know that better than anyone else."

"It was clever of you to use me for your alibi, Lew. But something has been bothering me since that night and I just recently remembered what it was."

Lew stared back at her, waiting for her to continue.

"Remember when we got to the home, you had me zip up the back of your costume, because you couldn't reach it."

"What does that have to do with anything?"

"When I saw you later in the day room dancing around, the zipper was down."

"So what? It sometimes works its way down when I move."

"There was a clasp on the zipper. It should have kept it in place."

"I still don't know how that means anything?" Lew scoffed.

"It means that you took the costume off at some point and put it back on again."

A glint of understanding was registering in Drum's watery eyes. His chin began to quiver.

"I think," Liz continued, "that you took off the suit, sneaked out of the home and went back to your house and killed Marlee."

"That's ridiculous," Lew's voice was rising to a higher pitch. "I was at the home all the time. Ask anyone there. They'll tell you."

"Oh, they probably will say so. I'm sure they thought you were there. At least they saw Scooby Doo."

Drum said nothing. He now knew there was no point in bluffing anymore. Liz continued. "That means that you had to have had an accomplice. Someone you could have let in from the back door. Someone who could have helped you unzip that costume. I believe your accomplice was Natalie Taylor and she switched places with you, while you, went home, did the deed, came back and changed back into the costume. The problem was, that your Natalie had already left the building before you could finish changing. So, you left the zipper unzipped. You probably didn't even think it was important. Even if someone noticed, they probably wouldn't see any significance to it."

Tears were streaming down the banker's face now. He dabbed at them. Then buried his face in his hands and sobbed.

After a moment, Liz said, "You did kill Marlee then, didn't you Lew?"

He nodded his head up and down, his face still covered by his hands.

"Were you also involved in what Martin Callan was into?" Liz asked.

Lew let his hands slip away from his face and placed them on the desk once more. He shook his head from side to side. "No. Not really. But I did know what he was up to. At least I was pretty sure of it. Martin knew I had been involved with both Jane Pruitt and Natalie. Then when Natalie did what she did, Martin suspected what had happened. He was furious with me. He was involved in a scheme with someone at the hospital and he was afraid that a murder investigation would bring attention to the hospital and might reveal what he'd been up to."

"And what had he been up to?" Liz quizzed.

"You just told me when you came in, Liz. You said it was money laundering."

Liz waited for more.

"Of course that's what I thought anyhow. He had been slowly moving that money for years. First he sent Roger to college and medical school and then he bought that farm equipment dealership."

"What money was that?"

Lew squirmed in his chair. "I don't know if you remember it. There was an armored car robbery some years back."

"Yes. Joe worked that case off and on for several years. The robbers and the money were never found."

"Yes, it was," Lew said. "I found it. Well found probably isn't the word. I saw Martin Callan hide the money in the old quarry. I was out hunting with a couple of other fellows that night. I had gotten separated from them and saw the armored car drive out into that open field. The armored car driver and the guard were in on the job. They met a third person who double crossed them. He killed them both and kept all the money for himself. I followed him to the old quarry and got close enough to see who it was,"

"Martin Callan," Liz supplied.

"Yes. He didn't see me. He thought he had pulled it off without a hitch."

"Why didn't you report it?"

"After he left, I took a look at the stash. It was an awful lot of money. I...I took one of the bags. I didn't think it would be missed."

"What did you do with it?" Liz asked.

"Nothing at first. I was afraid to. I kept going back to the quarry and checking on it. It hadn't been touched, so I figured Martin was letting it cool off. The third time I checked on the money, I took some more. That's what I used to start this bank. I never knew if Martin had ever realized that any of the money was missing."

"He must have," Liz said almost to herself. "He seemed to think that I had some of it. Last night, he demanded it from me." Then it occurred to her. "My God, he must have been the one who hurt Joe."

"I always suspected that he did. Joe must have found out about the quarry somehow. Maybe he even followed Martin. I don't know."

"And you never told anyone?" Bitterness crept into Liz's voice.

"No. I'm sorry, Liz."

Liz only glared at him. No he wasn't sorry she thought. At least not sorry enough. To think that she had considered this man to be a friend, when all the time, he let Joe's attacker run free. Just for his own selfish reasons.

"Do you know if Roger Callan was in on it too?"

"I don't think so. At least I never had an inkling that he did."

"Tell me, Lew," Liz asked. "Did you do the breakins?"

Lew nodded. Then after a moment, he said, "But I never meant to hurt you, I just wanted to make it all seem real."

"One more thing, I want to know, Lew." Her voice was cold and demanding this time. Gone was the sorrow she had felt for the man when she first came into his office. "Why? Why? Did you have to kill Marlee?"

Drum felt the iciness of Liz's stare. He looked straight into her face and his lips quivered. "I took care of that woman for years," he said. "She had one ailment after another. I took her to doctors. I cooked for her, I cleaned the house. I waited on her hand and foot. I cleaned up after her. Especially after that infernal bag she had to wear. It would leak and the smell and the mess were disgusting. It seemed like she was never going to get better. I was never going to be free to have a life. Then there was Natalie and after what she was willing to do for me, I knew I had to end it with Marlee. She wasn't having any quality of life anyways. I deserved a life too." His voice was becoming loud and shrill as if trying to make himself hear and understand. Then he lowered his voice and leaned across the desk, peering up into Liz's impassive face. "You just don't know what it's like to have to take care of someone like that day after day."

"No. I don't suppose I do," Liz said coldly. Then almost to herself she said in a low sad tone, "I guess I should ask Deb."

"Ask Deb? I don't think I understand."

"No Lew, I don't think you do."

"Well. What do you think, Liz?" Deb asked.

"About what?" Liz was sitting in her chair and stroking Sissy Boom Boom.

"Haven't you been listening to a word I said?" Deb came back with annoyance.

"Of course. Every word." Liz was tired. She had not taken a nap all day. She kept thinking about Lew Drum, Marlee, Martin Callan and Joe and couldn't settle herself down enough to be able to sleep. Mac had told her that Blakeney had been arrested and had been willing to talk. He had followed Shirley Robbins from the hospital and had hidden in her car, but he did not kill her. He had called Martin Callan and he had met them on the old quarry road. Callan had disposed of the girl.

Roger Callan had not been involved in his father's schemes and was devastated. Liz felt sorry for him and wondered if they could ever have a relationship again. She really hoped so.

"So. Then what do you think?" Deb pursued.

"About what?" Liz asked again.

"I knew you weren't listening," Deb pouted. "You never listen to me." Then she added, "But you will. Everybody in town is going to listen to me after I'm elected."

"Elected? What on earth are you talking about?"

"See? You weren't listening. I knew you weren't"

"For heaven's sake, Deb what is this all about?"

"I'm gonna run for town council. With Lew Drum and Martin Callan cooling their heels in the calaboose, there's two openings on the council. I figure I can snag at least one of them."

Liz laughed. "You going to fill two chairs at once? You keep eating ice cream like you do and maybe you can."

"Ha. Ha." Deb chided. "Don't you go making fun of me. I know I can't get two places on the council. I'm smarter than that."

"I'm sure."

"And don't go making cracks about me getting fat neither."

Liz just laughed.

"Go ahead and laugh," Deb said. "You'll be laughing out the other side of your face when I'm on the council."

"You on the council?" Liz said. "That's ridiculous."

"Mac don't think it's so ridiculous."

"So, now it's Mac with you too, is it? I take it you've changed your mind about our chief of police."

"Aw, I always thought he was a pretty good man. It was just that Sadie broad that was leading him astray. But I've straightened him out on that."

"Oh, you have, have you?"

"Darned right I have. And if he ever strays away from his wife again, you can be sure, it will be for me."

"Did he tell you that?"

"Not in so many words, but I can tell what a man thinks."

"So, Mac is encouraging you to run for council."

"He said with me on the town council, this town would never be the same again."

Liz nodded and smiled. "I can agree with that."

"Good I'm glad you see things my way. Now I'd better get busy on my campaign. She exited the living room and headed down the hall for her own room.

Liz reached for the candy dish on the coffee table and picked out a lollipop. She unwrapped it. Lemon. That figures, she thought. She put it in her mouth and stroked Sissy Boom Boom, saying to herself, "Then I guess the whole town better buckle their seat belts. Looks like it's going to be another bumpy ride."